"I need you Ysabel."

More than I ever thought possible. "And you owe me a two-week notice."

"Does everything have to be on your terms?"

"Damn right." She had him tied in a knot so tight he couldn't remember how to breathe. His hand curled around the back of her neck, feathering through the silky smooth hair falling down to her waist.

"Someone needs to teach you a lesson on compromise." Her own arms twined around his neck and she brought his mouth closer to hers.

He stopped a breath away from her lips. "And I know just the one who can do it." Then his lips closed over hers.

Two months hadn't been nearly long enough to erase Ysabel from his mind, hadn't been long enough to make him forget how she felt against him.

And his body remembered.

it crashed into the concrete. Then she dived out onto the ground,

Dear Reader,

This year marks the 60th anniversary of Harlequin Books. I am very excited and honored to be included in the ranks of Harlequin authors on such a special occasion.

When I was asked to be a part of the DIAMONDS AND DADDIES continuity in celebration of Harlequin's 60th anniversary, I jumped at the opportunity. I felt privileged to be included in the effort with other wonderful authors I've met and enjoyed reading. We worked as a team to dream up the world of the Aggie Four, the Texas locations and the plots. It was fun to see our stories unfold and come alive.

I grew up reading Harlequin romance novels, sneaking them from my mother's stacks of books to escape into another world of excitement, adventure and true love. As a teenager reading those wonderful stories, I never in my wildest dreams thought one day I'd be one of the authors. Yet here I am. It all goes to show you that dreams can come true and happily-ever-afters don't only happen in fairy tales.

Thank you for being a part of Harlequin's 60th anniversary. Happy reading!

Elle James

ELLE JAMES

BABY *Bling*

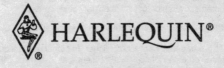

TORONTO • NEW YORK • LONDON
AMSTERDAM • PARIS • SYDNEY • HAMBURG
STOCKHOLM • ATHENS • TOKYO • MILAN • MADRID
PRAGUE • WARSAW • BUDAPEST • AUCKLAND

I'd like to thank the wonderful authors who contributed to bringing this continuity together, making it come alive with action, adventure and romance. None of this could have happened if not for our terrific editors for their support and belief in us as authors. A great big, special thanks to Harlequin for making my dreams come true.
Happy anniversary!!!

Recycling programs
for this product may
not exist in your area.

ISBN-13: 978-0-373-69394-8
ISBN-10:   0-373-69394-X

BABY BLING

Copyright © 2009 by Mary Jernigan

www.eHarlequin.com

Printed in U.S.A.

ABOUT THE AUTHOR

2004 Golden Heart Winner for Best Paranormal Romance, Elle James started writing when her sister issued a Y2K challenge to write a romance novel. She managed a full-time job, raised three wonderful children and she and her husband even tried their hands at ranching exotic birds (ostriches, emus and rheas) in the Texas Hill Country. Ask her and she'll tell you what it's like to go toe-to-toe with an angry 350-pound bird! After leaving her successful career in Information Technology Management, Elle is now pursuing her writing full-time. She loves building exciting stories about heroes, heroines, romance and passion. Elle loves to hear from fans. You can contact her at ellejames@earthlink.net or visit her Web site at www.ellejames.com.

Books by Elle James

HARLEQUIN INTRIGUE

906—BENEATH THE TEXAS MOON
938—DAKOTA MELTDOWN
961—LAKOTA BABY
987—COWBOY SANCTUARY
1014—BLOWN AWAY
1033—ALASKAN FANTASY
1052—TEXAS-SIZED SECRETS
1080—UNDER SUSPICION, WITH CHILD
1100—NICK OF TIME
1127—BABY BLING

CAST OF CHARACTERS

Jackson Champion—A self-made billionaire shipping tycoon whose shipping business and credibility are under attack. One of the original surviving members of the Aggie Four, he's capable of many things, but is he capable of terrorism?

Ysabel Sanchez—Jackson's executive secretary and prime support is on the verge of resigning to keep Jackson from finding out she's pregnant with his child.

Deke Norton—Successful owner of Norton International and former college classmate of Jackson's. Has he really overcome his envy of the Aggie Four's camaraderie and success?

Mitch Stanford—Married to Ysabel's cousin and a member of the sheriff's department. Can he help Jackson beat the terrorism charges?

Brody Green—The Harris County Sheriff's Department detective investigating Champion Shipping and the death of a forklift driver. How committed is he to protecting and defending the people of Harris County?

Greg Voleski—A quiet, mild-mannered and capable deckhand liked by most, but a loner with a secret past. Does he have reasons for remaining aloof?

Tom Walker—Management trainee and recent Texas A&M graduate, in the fast-track training program at Champion Shipping.

Flint McKade—Successful businessman, cowboy and owner of the Diamondback Ranch, a five hundred acre horse breeding and cattle ranch in Houston. A proud member of the Aggie Four.

Sheik Akeem Abdul—Successful businessman who owns a high-end horse auction business in Harris County, Texas. Although he spent four years in the Middle East, he considers the Aggie Four his family.

Viktor Romanov—The fourth member of the Aggie Four, he and his family were killed when their country was overthrown.

Jenna Nilsson—Jackson Champion's ex-fiancé, whom he caught cheating before the wedding.

Chapter One

Jackson Champion stood on the Bayport Container Yard loading dock, sleeves rolled up, his cowboy hat tipped back on his head. Overhead illumination eclipsed the moon, making the busy container yard brighter than day with light reflecting off the low ceiling of clouds.

Despite the solid concrete beneath his feet, Jackson's body still swayed to the rhythm of the ocean. It usually took more than twenty-four hours for him to get his land legs back after several weeks at sea. His two-month reprieve, delay of the inevitable, call it what it was—okay, escape was the right word—had come to an end.

The time had come to face the consequences of a night spent in Ysabel Sanchez's arms. Yet here he was delaying the face-to-face he owed her by sticking around to direct the off-loading of cargo from his ship. A task the stevedores and deckhands normally managed quite well without his presence.

Cranes lifted containers from the ship, stacking them in the container yard with artful precision. He didn't have to be there, but he told himself he wanted to supervise the unloading of the special cargo he'd shipped for his remaining friends and founding members of the Aggie Four Foundation, Flint and Akeem. Just one more delay tactic. A twinge of regret passed over Jackson. One of their four had died recently; the pain still ached like an open wound.

The crate full of expertly designed Rasnovian saddles would bring a good price at Akeem's auction. But the money wouldn't buy a replacement for Jackson's pending loss. An inevitable defeat from any angle he chose to view it.

The woman was sure to leave him. No doubt about it. She had every right. Hell, she had the right to sue him for sexual harassment if she wanted to get legal on him. Not that Izzy would do that. She was one classy lady, grown from the same stock as he was. The stock of hard knocks. A grin threatened to spill across his face. She hated being called Izzy.

No, Ysabel wouldn't sue; she'd walk out on him. The two months enforced reprieve could be viewed as running away from his problem—although the problems he'd encountered while away had needed his on-site decision power. Jackson chose to call it delaying the inevitable. He'd missed her and he'd miss her even more when she was gone entirely out of his life.

He rolled the kinks out his shoulders and located the stevedore superintendent, the one man on the dock with a clue as to where the container holding the saddles was located and when it would be unloaded.

Being the owner didn't make him any more anxious to interrupt the complicated task of unloading a cargo ship. Weight distribution meant everything to the successful completion of the task.

His skin twitched in the side of his jaw, impatience settling in like a case of poison ivy, making him want to scratch all over. Now that he was back in Houston, he was anxious to get to the office and see what had happened in his two-month absence from the corporation he'd built from the ground up, Champion Shipping, Inc. Everyone would have gone home for the evening, except perhaps Ysabel. If he could catch her alone, maybe he could apologize and promise not to let it happen again.

His groin tightened at just the thought of that one night of the most incredible sex he'd ever experienced. Rebound sex, he'd called it. And it could cost him his most valuable employee. Ysabel Sanchez—executive assistant, master planner and right-hand man…er, woman. Ysabel was the one person he could count on to ground him in reality, tell it like it was and pick the right tie for every occasion. Even in his absence, she managed the day-to-day operations without a snag. She'd kept his schedule straight, reminded him of his social obligations and arranged his itinerary long-distance. The woman was phenomenal in more ways than he could enumerate.

Then why was he so hesitant to head back to the office?

Because he knew as soon as they were face-to-face, she'd hand him her resignation and walk out. Ysabel wasn't a one-night-stand kind of woman. She'd want the happily-ever-after, something Jackson hadn't believed in since his mother left him and his father twenty-seven years ago.

And after the fiasco with his ex-fiancée, Jackson was even less inclined to commit to that particular lifestyle than before. Not that Ysabel was anything like Jenna Nilsson.

The stevedore superintendent, Percy Pearson, glanced his way, Jackson's cue he could ask his question without interrupting the man's concentration.

Jackson closed the distance and held out his hand to the man. "Percy, good to see you. Have you seen the container with the special cargo yet?"

The man checked his handheld cargo tracking device. "Unloaded fifteen minutes ago. Should be in the second row of containers in that section." He pointed to a row of containers on the dock.

"Thanks." Jackson strode to the end of the row and found the container marked "Special." When he circled behind the container, he noted the container door had been opened and part of the shipment had been removed. "What the hell?"

A forklift carrying a pallet with a crate on it headed away from the ship and the open container, moving faster than was authorized in the chaotic structure of the container yard.

"Mr. Champion? I'm Tom Walker, the super said I could find you here." A young man probably in his early twenties hurried up to Jackson. He wore a crisp new business suit and shiny black wing-tipped shoes, fresh off the shelves. "Miss Sanchez sent me over. I'm the new management trainee on the executive rotation."

Was this Ysabel's idea of a joke? Not that he had time to worry about it when someone had pilfered his goods. "Did you see that?" Jackson pointed to the forklift. "I think that forklift driver took off with my property."

"Was he supposed to?" Tom asked.

"No." Jackson's gut tightened, anger rocketing through his bloodstream the farther away the forklift moved.

"You want me to chase him?" Tom stared down at his wing tips and shrugged. "I could probably catch him if I was wearing my running shoes."

"No, I'll take care of it." Jackson ran for an idle forklift he'd spotted standing between the containers. He hopped aboard and in seconds had the machine running. With the skill of one who'd done his share of stevedoring in his younger days, he backed out of the containers and turned toward the disappearing forklift. With a flip of a lever, Jackson shifted into forward and pushed the accelerator all the way forward.

Before the forklift moved two yards, Tom jumped on the back and held on to the cage surrounding the seat.

"What are you doing?" Jackson asked.

"Miss Sanchez told me I should stick to you like glue, no matter what."

"She did, did she?" Jackson pushed the vehicle faster, swinging around the corner the other forklift had taken.

"Yes, sir. Wow! I didn't know this rotation would be this exciting!" he shouted over the whine of the engine pushing the forklift to its limits.

Jackson didn't know his return would be as eventful as his two-month trip. He could use a little calm and boredom about now.

The thief had a lead of at least a football field's length, maneuvering past containers and personnel, narrowly missing several longshoremen unhooking a pallet from a crane's cable.

The forklift made a sharp left turn, sliding between rows of neatly stacked containers in weathered shades of orange, red and silver.

Rage spurred on Jackson. When he reached the spot where the other forklift had spun to the left, he didn't slow down. His forklift skidded to the right, skinning the side of a metal container, the clash of metal on metal sending sparks flying.

"You all right back there?" Jackson called out, a quick glance back at the young man made him smile.

The guy's suit was dirty, his face smudged with grease from the forklift and his teeth shone white in a face-splitting grin. "I'm still here, aren't I?"

Jackson could admire a tough kid. "You passed your first test."

"Oh, yeah? What test is that?"

"Keeping up with the boss!" He poured on the juice and sent the forklift shooting forward, but he could no longer see the other machine. "Where the hell did he go?" Slowing his own vehicle, he was about to give up and get the police involved when a shout behind him made him jump.

"There!" From his perch on the back of the forklift, Tom could see farther. He waved his arm back behind him, jabbing his finger to the right. "He went down that aisle."

Jackson slammed the forklift in Reverse and spun around, heading back the way Tom pointed. Like the young man said, the runaway forklift was making tracks across the container yard and would have gotten away if not for Tom's sharp eyes and quick response.

As he closed in on the other forklift, Jackson prepared for a fight, but he didn't get the chance.

The forklift jerked to the left, crossing Jackson's path.

Jackson stomped the brake and swerved to the right.

The forklift skidded back to the right and then left. Clearly the driver had lost control and was headed straight for a container.

"Look out!" Jackson called out, but the forklift driver drove full speed into the twenty-foot container. A small explosion blasted wood crating and metal in all directions.

"Get down!" Jackson threw himself off the forklift and dragged Tom off the back. Before they could hit the ground, another explosion shook the earth as the propane tank on the wrecked forklift erupted in a fiery ball of flame.

"WELL?" Delia's voice carried through the wood paneling of the bathroom door.

Ysabel stared down at the wand, blood rushing from her head, making her dizzy. As she'd suspected, but prayed otherwise, a blue line.

"Izzy? Are you all right?" Delia's voice was soft but insistent, bringing tears to Ysabel's eyes. She'd need her sister more than ever now.

Given all the other signs, Ysabel shouldn't have been surprised at the results of the test, but she'd hoped that maybe she was wrong. Maybe she'd missed her period because of stress and maybe that same stress had caused her stomach to be upset every morning for the past month. Yeah, and maybe pigs could fly.

So she was pregnant. She'd handled bigger problems for Champion Shipping; she could handle the matter of a baby, no problem. Ysabel opened the door and holding the wand up for her sister to see, stepped out of the bathroom.

Delia squealed and hugged her sister so hard she couldn't breathe. "I'm so excited. I get to be an auntie!"

Ysabel pried her sister loose and stepped back. "I'm glad someone is excited. You know it changes everything."

Delia's smile stayed in place. "So? Is that such a bad thing?"

"Only when the baby happens to be Jackson Champion's." Ysabel turned and paced the short length of Delia's living room floor in her Houston apartment. "Jackson's back in town." She stopped and sucked in a long shaky breath. "Holy Mary Mother of God, I'm about to be jobless."

"And pregnant. Why resign now? It's just not like you to quit anything, *mi hermana*. You sure you want to give up the best job you'll ever have?"

"I can get another." Ysabel ran a hand through her sleek light-brown hair that had worked its way out of the normal tight ponytail at the nape of her neck.

"Paying as well as the rich *gringo* pays you?" Delia huffed. "Not likely."

"Don't call him *gringo*," Ysabel automatically defended, dropping her hands to her sides, her fists tightening almost as much as the knot in her gut. "I'll find another job."

"So when are you going to tell him?" Her sister's brows winged upward. "The man has the right to know."

"I know, I know. I just can't risk letting him find out until I get far enough away from him."

"You really think he'll sue for custody? A playboy like Jackson Champion?"

Ysabel snorted. "The man keeps what's his. How do you think he got so rich?" He kept everything but the women in his life. For some reason he seemed to go through women like an addict goes through drugs. As far as Ysabel knew, she'd been around longer than any of the females close to him because she hadn't slept with him. Up until she made the *Big Mistake*.

"Ysabel, a child is different. It'll only slow him down."

"Not if he hires a nanny to raise it."

"Madre de Dios!" Delia crossed her arms over her chest. "No niece of mine will be raised by a perfect stranger. She has more than enough family in the area to raise her properly."

A sad smile lifted the corners of Ysabel's lips. "If all goes as I intend, I won't be in this area much longer."

Delia's eyes glistened. "But where will you go? Mama will be devastated if she doesn't get to spoil her first grandchild."

"It can't be helped. I won't lose my baby to anyone and I refuse to let him live a disrupted life of joint custody. He deserves a chance to be normal."

"Without a father?"

A pang of regret hit Ysabel square in the chest. "You and I both know Jackson rides life in the fast lane. He doesn't slow down long enough to notice anything but the business."

"He took enough time to get engaged."

"Only because it was on his scheduled time line of 'things to do before I die.' *I* penciled that in on his goals sheet when he wasn't looking one day. The man wouldn't have bothered if I hadn't." He'd totally missed the point, too. Ysabel could still feel the pain of watching him court woman after woman to find one who could provide the right corporate-wife image. He'd thought he'd found it in Jenna Nilsson. The witch. He'd even had Ysabel order an engagement ring for the woman. Wow. She shook her head. The memory still made her chest ache.

"Still, he did get engaged," Delia offered, wincing when Ysabel glared at her.

"For what it was worth!" Ysabel threw her arms in the air. "She was cheating on him from day one with an old boyfriend."

"You knew?"

Heat filled her cheeks. "Yeah, but I didn't have the heart to tell him. The man is clueless when it comes to women. He deserved her."

"Wow, and here I thought you were in love with the guy."

"Emphasis on past tense." Ysabel tossed her long, straight hair behind her shoulder. "I'm so over him."

"Right, that's why we've been talking about him for the past…" Delia glanced at her wristwatch, "thirty minutes."

Anger surged in Ysabel's chest. "Of all people, I thought you'd understand." She grabbed her purse and keys. "I'm going back to my place."

"You mean you're going back to the office, don't you?" Delia stood and followed Ysabel toward the door. "I don't know why you bother to keep an apartment, you practically live at the office. What are you going to do when you aren't working there anymore?"

"I *don't* live at the office and I *am* going to my apartment," Ysabel lied. She'd thought of a few things she'd wanted to straighten in Jackson's office before he showed up bright and early tomorrow.

Delia rolled her eyes. "Whatever."

As she reached for the door, her BlackBerry phone sang out the tune to *Mission Impossible*, the one she'd assigned to Jackson Champion's phone number. Her heart leaped into her throat, threatening to choke off her air. Ysabel dug in her purse for the device. "Where is that damned thing?"

"Calm down. He'll just keep ringing until you answer."

"I am calm!" Her fingers curled around the smooth black rectangle and she jerked it from her purse. For a moment she stared down at the name displayed across the miniature screen. Jackson Champion. Her breath caught in her throat and her fingers froze.

"Tell him, Ysabel. Tell him he's going to be a father."

"No, I can't. I have to quit first."

"You owe him that much."

Ysabel's hands shook. "I can't."

"At least answer the phone." Delia reached over her sister's shoulder and punched the Talk button. Then she leaned back against the wall, her brows rising up her smooth forehead in challenge.

"Ysabel? Ysabel! Are you there?" Jackson's voice barked out from the phone, jerking Ysabel out of her stupor.

Her hands shook as she pressed the phone to her ear. "Yes, I'm here."

"I need you down on the Bayport Terminal ASAP."

"Tell him," Delia whispered.

With Delia staring at her like her gaze could bore a hole into her conscience and Jackson's voice sending goose bumps across her skin, Ysabel shook her head. "I can't."

"What do you mean you can't?" Jackson asked. "I need you here now! And set up a meeting with the Aggie Four— Flint McKade and Akeem Abdul—for first thing in the morning. We've got big problems."

Ysabel resisted the urge to pull out a pen and jot down his instructions on the handy notepad she kept in her purse. She took a deep breath and straightened. It was now or never. "I quit."

"You what?" Jackson shouted.

Ysabel held the phone away from her ear until Jackson stopped yelling. "You heard me. I quit."

"That's what I thought you said. I don't know what's going on, but quitting at this point in time is not an option. Get down to the terminal now!"

It was just like the man to ignore her when *she* wanted something. Ysabel's stubborn streak set in with a vengeance. "Maybe you didn't understand what I just said."

"I understood just fine. I also have an employment contract that requires you give me two weeks notice."

Jackson paused, breathing heavily in the phone. "Look, I've had a lousy voyage with a man gone overboard. You sent me a trainee when I just got back in town, a crate full of what I thought were Rasnovian saddles just exploded in front of me, I have a dead man lying at my feet and the police are trying to arrest me for murder. Either you get down here now or I'll sue you for breach of contract!"

Chapter Two

"I tell you, as far as I knew, the box contained hand-crafted Rasnovian saddles, not explosives." Jackson held his temper in check. Now was not the time for letting loose. Not with a rabid, foaming-at-the-mouth detective ready to accuse him of God knew what.

Detective Brody Green nodded toward the area surrounded in yellow crime scene ribbon, a snarling sneer lifting his upper lip. "Obviously, the box wasn't full of saddles. Our crime scene experts are leaning toward explosive detonators. Would you care to explain that?"

Jackson's back teeth ground together. "Champion Shipping doesn't transport explosives or detonators. Nowhere on my manifests was this indicated or I would have put a stop to it before it left the port of embarkation."

Brody's lips twisted into a mirthless smile. "Right. Still, I'll need to question you and all your employees involved in the loading and unloading of this particular ship. And I'll bet the Department of Homeland Security will want to talk with you as well."

"Fine. I have nothing to hide." Jackson ran a hand through his hair and looked around for the hundredth time. Where was Ysabel?

As if reading his mind, Tom, the executive rotation trainee, stared down at his watch. "She said she'd be here in twenty minutes. That was…twenty minutes ago." He looked across the container yard and grinned. "Just like clockwork. How does she do it?"

The skin on the back of Jackson's neck tingled. He didn't need Tom's words to tell him Ysabel was behind him. The day of reckoning had arrived and Jackson was no more prepared for it than he'd been two months ago. *Face the music, Champion.* Face it and lose her.

Sucking in a deep breath, he slowly turned.

Ysabel Sanchez strode across the heated concrete, her heels clicking, her long straight hair swaying around her shoulders in a curtain of light. Her full hips mesmerized him in the glare of the overhead lights.

Jackson's mouth went dry and his groin tightened. Two months should have erased all physical yearnings he might have had for his executive assistant. It worked for all the other women he'd dated since he'd escaped puberty.

Ysabel wasn't like the other women. She carried herself as if she were a Spanish queen, poker-straight, a haughty tilt to her chin, all business and no nonsense. Yes, that was the Ysabel he wanted to remember, but he had the other Ysabel branded in his mind and every nerve ending in his body since that night he'd spent in her arms.

Jackson had witnessed the softness and tenderness beneath the hard-core front she put on for Champion Shipping. Her Spanish heritage showed in the full curve of her breasts, the light olive tone of her skin and the rounded swell of her hips. Soft, moss-green eyes saw through his soul to the man he'd hidden beneath the rough exterior since his first day in the foster care system. The woman had a knack for reading minds. If Jackson believed in magic, Ysabel Sanchez was most definitely a witch.

His hands ached for the straight, light brown hair that

sifted through his fingers like strands of the finest silk. Beneath that cool, professional exterior lurked a fiery passion he hadn't seen before. The urge to pull her into his arms and pick up where they'd left off that night in his bed nearly blew away his icy reserve. Damn the woman to hell!

Jackson suppressed a moan and struggled to keep his hands in his pockets and maintain a professional face in front of the detective and the kid. Neither of them had a need to know of his transgression or his secret lust for his executive assistant. That was his cross to bear.

Without a "Hello" or a "Good to see you" after two months out of the office, Jackson skipped the niceties and went straight for dealing with the more immediate problem. "Detective Brody, Ysabel Sanchez."

Ysabel extended a graceful hand. "Detective."

The detective's eyes narrowed, his lips tightening. "Miss Sanchez." He didn't take her hand, just raised his notepad a degree and made a show of jotting down notes with the government black pen. "For the record, what is your relationship to Mr. Champion?" His glance skewered her.

Sensing the detective's rising ire, Jackson jumped in and answered for Ysabel. "Miss Sanchez is my executive assistant."

"Right." Detective Brody's gaze swept her from head to toe. "We should all have our very own *assistant* like Miss Sanchez, shouldn't we?" A nasty smile slid across his face as he glanced at Jackson and Tom.

Tom's brows rose and Jackson's anger spiked to dangerous.

"Don't overstep your boundaries, Detective," he warned, his fists clenching at his sides. If the man wasn't sporting a badge and a gun, Jackson would have taken a swing and to hell with the consequences.

But with a man being loaded onto a gurney for transportation to the morgue and an unexplained shipment of explosives, Jackson couldn't afford to lose his cool. No matter how warranted.

Ysabel's lips spread in a tight smile, her hand dropping to her side. "Could someone fill me in on what's going on?" She glanced up at Jackson, her gaze quickly shifting to Tom.

A twinge of annoyance made Jackson's chest tighten. So things weren't right with her either after the two-month absence. So much for time and distance diminishing memories. Damn, he had a lot of backpedaling to do to convince Ysabel not to leave Champion Shipping. And he had to. She'd become his lifeline to sanity in a business that seemed to have mushroomed overnight.

Detective Brody stepped between Jackson and Ysabel, completely ignoring her and addressing only Jackson. "Could you direct me to whoever is in charge of offloading the cargo from your ship?"

Longing for a minute or two with Ysabel to set the record straight—although a minute wouldn't be nearly enough—Jackson grit his teeth. "Sure." He turned to Tom. "Could you enlighten Miss Sanchez? I'll be back." He hoped.

"Yes, sir." Tom practically snapped to attention at the request.

A small smile quirked the corners of Ysabel's mouth.

Warmth filled Jackson's chest. That was the easy smile he remembered from his assistant before he'd slept with her. The warmth chilled almost as quickly as it came on. What he wouldn't give to put things back to the way they were.

He walked away, leading the detective toward Percy Pearson, the superintendent responsible for offloading the cargo.

All the while, he could feel her gaze boring into his back. Yeah, he'd screwed up. If only he could get her alone and try to undo the mistake and make things right again.

Fat chance.

YSABEL clutched her purse to keep her hands from shaking. Her first face-to-face contact with the man who had tied her in knots for the past two months hadn't gone nearly as she'd planned. She'd wanted to get him alone, hand over her resignation letter and walk out. A clean break. The less said the better. After he'd walked—no, make that ran—from his apartment following the most incredible night of sex she'd ever experienced, she had a firm understanding of what he expected from her.

Nothing. And she should expect nothing from him.

She might have been able to hide her true feelings and gone on, business-as-usual just like she had for the past two months—which hadn't been hard considering the man had disappeared off the face of the earth physically, if not so much by e-mail and voicemail. Unfortunately, the result of their mental lapse in their otherwise professional relationship was the baby growing in Ysabel's womb.

Her hand rose involuntarily to her still-flat midsection. She'd harbored more than a professional yearning for her boss pretty much since she'd gone to work for him five years ago. Determined to keep her job, she'd squelched her natural desires and pretended that his constant parade of different women didn't hurt. After a while she'd begun to see a pattern in his dating. Date twice and dump. The women he dated were primarily money-hungry gold-diggers, mostly interested in his wealth and social standing. They hadn't been given a chance to know the man beneath the charming, if somewhat distant, exterior.

Being his assistant, Ysabel saw what made Jackson Champion tick. When he didn't think she was looking or he didn't notice she was in the room, she saw what made him hurt and knew more than he'd ever tell her about himself by simply observing. In order to better understand her boss, she'd done a little digging of her own and knew he didn't have family. Tossed into the foster care system at the sensitive age of seven, he'd been passed from one family to the next, never feeling the love of parents.

When he'd been more than a bear to work for, Ysabel reminded herself that the man had to be hurting inside still, never having resolved issues of loneliness and neglect from his childhood.

The only family he claimed was the Aggie Four, the close-knit group of friends he'd made while attending college at Texas A&M. An unlikely group of young men brought together by hard times, their own isolation and a need for friendship. He'd die for any one of them and they'd do the same.

A wave of sadness washed over Ysabel. The Aggie Four was now down to three. Even after three months, Viktor Romanov and his family's deaths still burned in her chest. She could imagine how Jackson felt. As his assistant, Ysabel had been involved in many meetings of the Aggie Four and come to know the men Jackson valued as friends on a more personal basis.

The young prince of Rasnovia had struggled to bring his country into the future. With the help and financial support of the Aggie Four Foundation, they'd combined forces to rebuild the small nation after its split from Russia. Democracy and capitalism had been introduced and flourished until a group of rebels overran the Romanovs, killing them and plunging the country into civil war.

A lot had happened in the past few months to all of the Aggie Four. She suspected it was more than coincidence. She sucked in a deep breath and turned to Tom, a smile spreading across her face. "So, how was your first day with the great Jackson Champion?"

Tom grinned. "Wow, the man's a dynamo! I'd no sooner gotten here then he was leaping onto a forklift and chasing after another." He filled her in on what had happened with the runaway forklift driver and the ensuing explosion.

"Any idea what caused the explosion?"

Tom's smile faded. "The firefighters found evidence of detonators in the debris. The detonators might have set off the propane tank on the forklift. The man driving…" Tom shook his head. "Not pretty."

The wind shifted, pushing the damp smell of charred wood and flesh toward Ysabel. Her stomach lurched. She'd had only two bouts of nausea in the past two weeks. That plus the missed period had clued her into the fact she might be pregnant. She pressed a hand to her mouth and willed her stomach to behave.

Jackson stalked back toward Ysabel and Tom, his face set in tight lines. "Detective Brody is breathing fire and trying to come up with reasons to throw me in jail."

Ysabel swallowed hard, hoping her stomach would stay down. "Why?"

"He wants to pin the shipment of detonators on me and Champion Shipping, not to mention slapping a murder charge on me for the thief's death." Jackson ran his hand through his hair, making the dark locks stand on end. "I'll need that emergency meeting of the Aggie Four to happen first thing tomorrow morning."

She nodded, afraid to open her mouth. Another waft of pungent air hit her and her stomach burbled.

"We'll meet at McKade's ranch house. I could use the fresh air." He glanced around the container yard, shaking his head. "If the Department of Homeland Security sinks its teeth into this, it could shut down Champion Shipping indefinitely."

Ysabel knew they could and she understood the impact to their customers and cash flow. They could lose millions.

"The detective said I could go but to expect more questions." Jackson turned to Tom. "Did you drive your own car?"

"Yes, sir."

"No need for you to ruin your night. I'll see you tomorrow in the office."

Tom nodded, shooting a look from Jackson to Ysabel for confirmation.

Ysabel nodded. "See ya tomorrow."

"Okay, then." Tom gave them one last look as though he was afraid he'd miss something important or exciting by leaving, then he turned and strode toward the parking lot.

Alone at last, Ysabel quelled an urge to run after Tom. She didn't want to be alone with Jackson. So much remained unsaid and even though she'd wanted to clear the air, now that she had the opportunity, she couldn't find the backbone to make it happen.

Jackson fixed that for her. He took one more look around then headed off toward the parking lot, his pace eating the distance. "Come on, I want to swing by the office. I'll need a list of all employees working the shipment here and in Rasnovia where we picked up the saddles. Then we'll need to compile a list of anyone who might have it in for me, although I suspect that could be a long one. You don't make as much money as I do without accumulating enemies."

"I know this isn't a good time for you, but what part of 'I quit' didn't you understand?"

Jackson stopped dead still. He didn't turn, didn't look at her, but his shoulders stiffened. "And what part of 'lawsuit' didn't you understand? I need you now to help me figure out this mess. After that, we'll discuss your severance options." He didn't wait for her response, but continued toward the parking lot.

Ysabel hurried to keep up. She was used to racing after Jackson even on a good day. He didn't waste time and he didn't suffer slowpokes. If only her stomach would cooperate. Several steps brought her closer to the source of the smell and she saw the emergency personnel zipping the remains of the forklift driver into a body bag.

The charred skin and the stench of burned flesh sent Ysabel over the edge. Her stomach heaved. She dropped back and held her hand over her mouth. *No, please, not now.* Tears welled in her eyes.

Jackson, aware he'd lost her, stopped and turned, a frown creasing his brow. "Is everything all right, Miss Sanchez?"

She wanted to throw something at him and hug him at the same time. Damn the man! Of course everything wasn't *all right.* And she couldn't tell him why. She could only hope that she didn't disgrace herself in front of him. Now would *not* be the time to display weakness. "I'm fine. Just winded," she lied and quickly clamped her hand back over her mouth.

Unconvinced, he retraced his steps and stood in front of her. "Are you feeling well?"

His concerned tone pushed the tears over the edge of her eyelids. They made a trail down her cheeks. She couldn't move, couldn't straighten fully without losing the contents of her stomach. Damn, why had she eaten that pizza with her sister? If she never saw another pizza again, it would be too soon.

Jackson's fingers clamped around her wrist and he tugged her hand down. "What's wrong Ysabel? Why the tears?" He scanned her face and looked down at her bare lips. "Your face and lips are pale. Perhaps you should sit down. Do I need to have the emergency personnel check you out?"

"No!" Her eyes widened. Fear he'd find out her secret made her reply more sharply than she'd intended. "No, I'm fine. Really. I must have eaten something that didn't agree with my stomach." Beads of perspiration sprang up on her brow. If only he'd back off and leave her to handle her *problem* on her own.

Jackson pushed a strand of hair behind her ear. "I think you should see the EMT." He glanced behind her.

Afraid he'd wave down one of the emergency responders, Ysabel straightened, pulling her hands out of his and swallowing the bile rising in her throat. "No, really." She smoothed her hands down her skirt and forced a smile. "See? I'm better already."

His frown deepened as though he didn't believe her for a minute. Then he shrugged. "Okay, then let's get out of here."

Holy Mary, Mother of God, that smell! A gentle gust of coastal wind pushed the horrible smell across Ysabel's nostrils and she was a goner.

Her stomach upended, regurgitated pizza and apple juice launching from her insides. Poor, unsuspecting Jackson, who still stood directly in front of her, didn't have a chance.

She emptied the contents of her miserable gut on his trouser legs and shoes.

Jackson yelped and jumped back, but not soon enough to avoid her unplanned aim.

Unable to stop, Ysabel retched and retched, tears squeezing from between her tightly shut eyelids.

Then she felt hands pulling her hair back behind her head and warm fingers holding her shoulders. The same hands that had stroked every inch of her body with such smooth sensuality, now held her gently, providing support and comfort.

Jackson's tenderness did nothing to stem the flow of tears coursing down her face. If anything it only made them worse.

When her stomach let up, she was able to ease to an upright position. Embarrassed and certain she was an undignified disaster, Ysabel turned her back to Jackson. "Leave me alone," she moaned.

"I can't." He turned her toward him and patted her face with a clean cotton handkerchief, drying her tears and mopping up what he could of her gastronomic pyrotechnics.

"I'm sorry. I guess the smell got to me."

He smiled and smoothed her hair back from her face. "It happens to the best of us."

"But not to me." Ysabel grabbed his wrist and relieved him of the scrap of cloth, her lips pressing into a tight line. She couldn't take much more of his concern. Not when she had to get away from him and Champion Shipping forever. Not when her heart was shattering into a billion pieces.

What a dope. How could she be so stupid to fall so completely in love with her boss?

Chapter Three

Jackson insisted on driving Ysabel's compact red car with its sparkling set of rosary beads dangling from the rearview mirror, folding his six-foot-two-inch frame behind the driver's wheel. After tossing her cookies at the container yard, Ysabel was too shaky and weak to maneuver Houston traffic—or so Jackson reasoned after wrestling the keys from her stubborn, unwilling hands.

Truth was, his own hands were shaking and he wasn't feeling so steady. Not that he'd ever admit it. The great Jackson Champion had narrowly missed being blown up and faced the possibility of going to jail all upon return from a two-month sabbatical from his home in Houston. But what had him confused and shaking inside was Ysabel being so violently ill.

Ysabel, the one constant in his life. The person he'd come to depend on for just about everything. The woman he'd betrayed by taking her to his bed in a fit of rebound sex.

His hands gripped the wheel so tightly that his knuckles whitened. Late at night the traffic in Houston was almost tolerable. He didn't have to sit in jammed lines of vehicles and pray his car didn't overheat in the unrelenting Texas sun.

"I thought we were going back to the office." Ysabel sat beside him, her normal color almost returned to her face, back in professional mode and ready to take on any challenge. She was amazing.

And that was the problem. She didn't know when to take time out for herself. She'd let him drive her into the dirt before she cried uncle. His lips pressed together. Wasn't it time to take others into consideration for once? Had he been that incredibly selfish? "I'm taking you back to my place."

"No!"

Her sharp reply made him risk a glance her way. In the light from the dash, her eyes rounded and she gripped her purse like the rail on the edge of a sheer drop-off. Was she scared of him?

The muscles in his chest pulled tight, especially the big one conducting blood through his system. He'd done that. Made her afraid of him, but that didn't change the fact she'd thrown up in the container yard and that he didn't think she should be left alone. "You're not well."

"Now that my stomach is empty, I feel just fine. Let's get to the office and pull up that information you wanted. I can't—don't want to go to your place…." Her voice trailed off and she chewed on her lip.

Jackson's teeth ground together. She didn't trust him to keep his hands to himself. He couldn't blame her. After all, he'd taken advantage of her giving nature two months ago and taken her to his bed. He shouldn't expect her to warm to the idea of being alone with him in the place he'd slept with her.

It had all unraveled because of his stupid, selfish attitude. So his ego had taken a hit after being jilted by his fiancée. He'd had no right to demand Ysabel meet him at his place after office hours. He'd been so obsessed with finding out why he'd been summarily dismissed by Jenna without so much as an explanation. It completely set him aback. Why would any woman walk away from marriage to a billionaire?

Ysabel tried to make him see that he hadn't been marrying for the right reasons. Love had never entered the equation with Jenna. He'd decided he needed a wife and Jenna had seemed to fit the bill.

Ysabel had argued that good breeding stock, with connections in the corporate world wasn't enough to base a marriage on.

He'd countered that he didn't want children nor the messiness and entanglement of love. No one ever won when love was involved. All he wanted was a wife to grace his dinner table when he entertained his important guests.

Ysabel had been equally passionate that love and family meant everything and that he should be glad Jenna called it off before Jackson had made the biggest mistake of his life.

Ysabel's green eyes had flashed with her zeal. Having called her to his condo late at night, she'd come immediately, dressed in a jean skirt and a skimpy camisole.

For the first time in their five-year relationship as employee and boss, Jackson saw past the professional facade she donned every day, and he was shocked. Shocked and completely and irrevocably turned on. Ysabel wasn't the sensible, icy exec he'd thought she was. She was fiery and sassy, strong and determined.

That's when he'd kissed her. The kiss led to more until he woke up the next morning with her lying next to him in his bed.

He'd come awake staring down at her, thinking how right she looked with her light brown hair splayed across his pillow, and how he could get used to having her wake up next to him every day of his life.

Then reality hit him like a rockslide. He'd steered clear of relationships for a reason. They never worked. Divorce happened and kids were abandoned and grew up in broken homes or foster homes. Like him.

He couldn't do that to any kid of his, couldn't bring a child into the world knowing he might not be in his life to give him the love and support he'd need. Knowing that most marriages were doomed to failure.

"Okay, then, I'm taking you home. You don't need to be working when you're sick."

"Really, I'm fine." She reached out and laid her hand on his arm.

An electric shock ran from where she touched all the way through him, making his heartbeat increase, pumping blood like an overworked piston through his bloodstream. His gaze dropped to where her slender fingers curled around his sleeve.

As quickly as she'd placed it there, she withdrew her hand and clasped it in her lap, pleating the fabric of her linen skirt, clearly nervous in his company.

What a mess he'd made of his relationship with the only woman he'd ever trusted. He'd destroyed her trust.

"I don't want to go home," she insisted. "We need to work quickly to get this matter resolved."

A heavy lump settled in his gut and his jaw tightened. "So you can resign?" He took a turn a little faster than he'd intended, tires skidding on the still-hot pavement.

"*Madre de Dios,* Jackson! Could you slow it down? I'm not partial to getting car sick and I don't relish being involved in a wreck."

"Sorry." He slowed, taking the turns at a reasonable speed, recognizing the physical effort it took him to keep his foot from ramming the accelerator through the floorboard. Once he'd eased onto Interstate 45 heading into downtown Houston, he willed his fingers to loosen their grip.

"In answer to your previous question…" She sighed. "Yes. Partly. I want to have this situation resolved before I leave the corporation. More than that I want to stop whoever is using Champion Shipping to smuggle deadly and illegal substances." Her hands balled into fists. "We need to nail the bastard."

A smile pushed Jackson's lips up on the edges. That was his Ysabel. She had been the most loyal employee on his payroll, doing everything in her power to ensure the success of Champion Shipping.

"Thanks." He shot a glance her way. "I guess that's all I can expect."

Her shoulders rose and fell on a deep breath. "Jackson, we need to talk."

The lead weight in his gut flipped. "We need to talk" always meant she needed to say something and he wasn't going to like it. He risked another glance her way, trying to read the expression in her profile and failing miserably. Out of the far corner of his eye, he caught a flash of headlights glaring off his side mirror. Before he could turn and look, a dark sedan raced up beside the compact car and slammed into the driver's side.

Having relaxed his grip on the wheel, Jackson wasn't prepared for the impact. The car jolted and skidded to the side, bounced against the concrete guard rail and swerved across three lanes of traffic. The dark sedan slammed into the back panel, setting the car into a spin.

"Holy Jesus!" Ysabel cried out, bracing her hands against the dash.

Jackson fought to regain control of the car, bringing it to a hair-raising stop on the far shoulder against a concrete barricade, facing oncoming traffic.

The smell of burned rubber and exhaust fumes filled the interior of the small car.

Ysabel scrambled for the door handle, frantically trying to unlock it.

"Stay in the car, Izzy." He grabbed her hand, stopping her crazed attempt to get out. "We don't know if that guy will come back and hit us again."

"I don't care. I have to get out." She flung the door open and it crashed into the concrete. Then she dived out onto the ground.

Jackson jumped out and rounded the car.

Ysabel crouched on her hands and knees heaving, her entire body shaking with the effort. But nothing came up. The sound of her tortured gasps tore at Jackson's heart.

He dropped to the ground and gathered her against him. "Izzy, sweetheart, breathe." He sat back on the pavement, settling her in his lap. "Breathe, baby."

Her pale face glowed in the moonlight, her cheeks shining with tears. "I'm sorry."

"What have you got to be sorry about? I should have been paying attention."

"I'm not usually sick."

"I know, and that has me worried. I'm taking you to the hospital."

She stiffened. "No."

"I won't take no for an answer." He climbed to his feet, carrying Ysabel with him. "We're going to the hospital. This isn't right."

"No. I'll refuse treatment. Just take me home."

"Okay, so no hospital. But you're going home and I'm calling in my physician. End of subject."

She stared at him, her face close enough to kiss, her eyes rounded, with dark smudges beneath them.

The need to take her lips was more than an urge, it was an obsession. If he didn't think she'd slap his face, he'd have followed his desire. But Ysabel had had more than enough excitement for one day. He set her in the car and strapped on her seat belt, adjusting her seat back so that she lay fully reclined. "Don't worry about a thing. I'll take care of you."

An hour later, Jackson had reported the hit and run to the police and managed to get the corporate physician to pay a house call at Ysabel's apartment. With Jackson pacing the floor of her compact living room, Ysabel lay on her bed behind her closed bedroom door, a cold stethoscope pressed to her chest, willing the doctor to declare her fit and get the hell out.

Dr. Adams folded his stethoscope and shoved it into his bag. "How long have you known?"

"Known what?" Ysabel asked, her gaze darting to the closed door of her bedroom. Could Jackson hear their words through the wooden panels? She couldn't afford for him to find out now. She had to think, make plans and get the hell out of Houston.

"It doesn't take a brain surgeon to figure this out." Jackson's corporate physician smiled as if making a joke. "You've missed a period and you're throwing up, otherwise you're perfectly healthy."

She buttoned her shirt and climbed off the bed, putting distance between them. "I don't know what you're talking about."

"I've done the math. Question is, have you?" He waited, unmoving.

She teetered on the edge of lying again, but she'd had enough lying. "How accurate are home pregnancy tests?" Ysabel asked, her voice a soft whisper.

"They've been pretty accurate as long as you've gone past a period. I take it you've tested positive for pregnancy?"

Ysabel spun, a finger to her lips. "Shhh! I don't want anyone to know."

"You mean you don't want Jackson to know?"

"That's not what I said," she argued, her words guarded, her brows drawing together. The doctor had guessed about her pregnancy, would he also guess the father of the child to be Jackson Champion?

Dr. Adams laid a hand on her shoulder. "You don't have to worry. I respect doctor–patient confidentiality. Your secret is safe with me."

"Thanks." Ysabel swallowed the vile taste of guilt and nodded. "What are you going to tell Mr. Champion?"

"I'll tell him it *might* have been a mild case of food poisoning and that you'll be fine. Not the truth but not exactly a lie." He squeezed her shoulders in a reassuring grip. "Ysabel, I hope you have the good sense to let the father in on your secret. A man has a right to know he's got a child on the way."

She stared up into the man's eyes, tears forming in her own. After a long pause, she dipped her head. "I will." As soon as she knew how she could retain custody when the father of her child could buy half of Houston with the amount of money he had.

"Fair enough." Dr. Adams opened the door and stepped out into Ysabel's small living area decorated in bold shades of red, yellow and orange. "She's fine, Jackson. Nothing a good night's sleep won't cure."

"But why was she throwing up?"

"Hard to say without blood tests, probably food poisoning, but it appears as if the worst has passed."

"Don't you think we should take her to the hospital and run those blood tests?" Jackson stared over Dr. Adams's shoulder to where Ysabel stood in the doorway.

Butterflies turned somersaults in Ysabel's stomach. "I told you it was nothing. We don't need to waste any more of the doctor's time or burden the hospital with nothing but a little bit of food poisoning. Go home, Mr. Champion. Like the doctor said, I could use a little rest."

Jackson's forehead furrowed. "I'm staying."

"If you stay, I'm sure to get no rest at all." As soon as the words came out of her mouth, Ysabel realized how they could be misinterpreted and her face heated. "Just leave. I'll be at work bright and early in the morning."

"Take the day off. I can survive without you for a day." He plunked his cowboy hat on his head. "I don't like leaving you."

"*Madre de Dios!* You don't live here and I haven't invited

you to stay. So get out." She softened her words with a twisted smile.

The doctor nodded. "Leave the girl alone and go home, Jackson. She'll be fine."

His steps dragging, Jackson allowed the doctor to escort him out of Ysabel's apartment. Not until the door was closed behind them and their footsteps faded down the hallway, did Ysabel let out the breath she'd been holding.

If she'd known that was what it would be like to see Jackson again, she'd have asked him to stay away longer. Too tired to think, she stripped, took a quick shower and fell into her bed.

As her eyes closed, she thought of all that had happened in the past three hours.

She'd learned she was pregnant, tendered her resignation, Jackson had nearly been killed and they'd almost been run off the road by a homicidal maniac.

Yup, that pretty much summed up the day. She yawned, wondering what was in store for the next morning. Reaching down, she pulled the sheet up over her head as though that would keep the chaos away.

"FLINT? It's Jackson. We need to meet."

Dr. Adams had given him a ride back to the building he owned in downtown Houston where he had the penthouse condo on the twenty-fifth floor. He preferred the wide-open spaces of his ranch west of Houston, but his business necessitated a residence in the city.

Standing at the floor-to-ceiling window in nothing but his boxer shorts, he pressed the cell phone to his ear.

"Do you know what time it is?" Flint McKade grumbled into his ear.

"Two in the morning. I know it's late and I'm sorry to wake you, but I've got some serious problems. I'm going to need the help of the Aggie Four." His hand tightened as it hit him in a fresh wave of anger and sorrow that the Aggie Four was down to three now. Viktor's loss hit him harder when he needed the full support of the friends he'd grown to love and respect. He missed Viktor.

As much as he missed his dead friend, he needed the support of the ones still living. If he didn't find out who planted the detonators in that container, he'd not only be up on charges of murder for the death of the forklift driver, but he'd also be the prime suspect in the possible plot to commit an act of terrorism against the United States.

"What's the problem? Want me to come now?" Flint's voice perked up, all sleepiness vanishing.

"No, that's not necessary. Contact Akeem and let him know we're having an emergency meeting tomorrow at your ranch at noon."

"Will do." Flint paused. "You know we're with you, buddy, whatever the problem. Hang in there. There's nothing we can't overcome." That had been their mantra throughout school at Texas A&M. The mantra had followed them through the years of building their empires.

Jackson's throat tightened. He hoped they could overcome this mess, which right now seemed insurmountable.

FROM the rented apartment on the twenty-third floor, a man stood in darkness, staring through his binoculars at the building two blocks away. Things were going according to plan. The Department of Homeland Security would be heating up and all indications should point to the three remaining members of the Aggie Four.

Jackson Champion stood silhouetted against the window of his condo, unashamed of his nakedness and unaware he was being watched at that very moment. He appeared to be talking on his cell phone. Probably talking to one of his cronies about the accident at the terminal.

The hit and run on the interstate wasn't part of the plan, but he chalked it up to an added bonus. Jackson ought to be feeling the squeeze by now. If not, he would be soon.

Chapter Four

"Tom, I need you to scan the employee files of the ship that delivered that cargo yesterday. I want a list of all the employees, their backgrounds and the date they started work for Champion Shipping."

"Yes, ma'am." Tom sat behind his desk outside Ysabel's office and logged on to the computer. "I heard about the accident on the freeway last night. I'm glad no one was injured."

"Yeah." So was Ysabel. They had been too close to death for her liking. Now that she was carrying a baby, she had to be more careful—think of someone beside herself in the equation.

She paced the floor of her office, having arrived later than intended. For the first time in the five years she'd worked for Champion Shipping, she just couldn't drag herself out of bed at her usual five o'clock in the morning. Partly because of the late night at the terminal and mostly because of the exhaustion of the first trimester of pregnancy.

She'd Googled pregnancy online and read about it while nibbling on crackers, hoping to keep her stomach down when every little smell set her off. All she needed was to throw up in front of Jackson again and he'd have an ambulance there so fast she wouldn't know what hit her. No, she had to keep her morning sickness from him at all costs. The best way would be to avoid him altogether.

"Miss Sanchez!" Jackson bellowed from the corner office next to hers.

So much for avoiding the man. As she left her office, she paused, staring at Tom, trying to think of a way to keep from being alone in the same room with Jackson. At the rate she was going, he'd have her secret figured out. A man who'd accumulated as much wealth as Jackson had wasn't a complete moron. She smiled at the younger man. "Tom, will you go see what Mr. Champion wants and tell him I had to run an errand?"

Tom cast a glance toward the billionaire's office, a frown furrowing his unlined forehead. "Are you sure? He called for you."

Guilt smacked her in the gut. She reasoned that the consequences of Jackson learning about her secret outweighed the guilt in her conscience.

"Miss Sanchez!"

Ysabel jumped and rolled her eyes. "*Fine.* I'll see what the man wants." She trudged her way toward his office, her feet dragging with every step. With her hand on the doorknob, she squared her shoulders and pushed the door wide. "Mr. Champion, is there something I could get you?"

"I thought I told you to take the day off." He stood with his arms crossed over his chest, his feet wide, his back to the glass windows that were openly displaying a gloriously bright morning in downtown Houston.

Ysabel blinked, trying to read Jackson's expression. The glare of light from the windows effectively cast his face in the shadows and more likely exposed every line, crease and smudge of her own face in minute detail. From the glance in her bathroom mirror that morning, she wasn't looking her best. Far from it. "If it makes you feel better, I slept in. I just got here."

His eyes narrowed and she squirmed under his inspection. "How are you feeling this morning?"

She pushed her lips into a cheerful smile she didn't nearly

feel. "Completely fine." *As long as I don't look at food before noon.*

He stared at her hard for another ten seconds before his arms fell to his sides. Jackson dropped into the plush leather seat behind the massive desk crafted by an artist in south Texas from the finest mesquite available in the state. "Good, then I'll need you to come with me when I meet with the Aggie Four at noon.

Her breath caught in her throat and she swallowed to clear it. "Here in Houston?" She crossed her fingers behind her back, praying the group would meet nearby, otherwise she'd be stuck in Jackson's truck, alone with the man for the forty-five minutes to an hour it took to reach the ranch west of Houston.

"We're meeting at the Diamondback. Be ready to go in forty-five minutes." His focus shifted to the papers requiring immediate attention on his desk, his attitude one of dismissal.

Grateful for the respite, Ysabel turned toward the door. Before she could exit, two men stepped into the doorframe, blocking her path.

"Mr. Jackson?" The first one crossed the threshold.

Ysabel recognized him as Detective Brody Green from the container yard the previous evening. Her chest tightened. Why would they come to Champion Shipping instead of having Jackson come to them to give his statement?

Instead of slipping out of the office to leave Jackson alone, she stepped back and allowed the lawmen to enter.

Jackson stood. "Detective Green, I hope you have some good news for me."

The man's mouth tightened. "Sorry, Mr. Champion. Can't say that I have." He jerked his head toward the man beside him. "Fielding?"

The man stepped forward, his hand extended to Jackson.

"Mr. Champion, I'm Special Agent Bob Fielding, with the Federal Bureau of Investigations. I'm working this case in conjunction with the Department of Homeland Security."

Ysabel's heart dropped to her stomach. Was the other shoe about to fall? Would they shut down Champion Shipping?

"Mr. Fielding. What can I do for you?" Jackson asked, his voice polite, his expression that of an expert poker player.

The agent withdrew a pad and pen from his jacket pocket. "I have a few questions for you regarding the explosion yesterday. That and I regret to inform you that we'll have to shut down the offloading of the remaining cargo on your ship until it has been thoroughly examined." Fielding tapped his pen to his note pad. "This incident, the radiation-poisoning incident at the Diamondback Ranch, plus the explosion and deaths of three men on one of your airplanes raises a boatload of other questions for the Aggie Four Foundation. Oh, and I also heard that you had a man go overboard on the sail across the ocean."

Jackson's face remained unflinching, his gaze shifting from Agent Fielding to Detective Green. The only indication of his ire was the muscle twitching in his jaw.

Familiar with his ability to hide all emotion, Ysabel picked up on the dangerous level of anger brewing beneath the surface. She stepped forward in hopes of diffusing the situation. "Do you have any idea how long the investigation will take? You do understand that time is money. By shutting down the offloading of the ship, you tie up the berth for longer than originally contracted."

"I'm sorry, Miss—" Fielding glanced from Jackson to Ysabel.

Ysabel redirected his attention to her by shoving a hand in his direction. "I'm Ysabel Sanchez, Mr. Champion's executive assistant. Do we need to call in our legal staff?"

Fielding's brows rose with his shoulders. "That might be

a possibility. We have four agents assigned to the ship along with two sniffing dogs. We should be able to complete our scan in a day. Two tops."

"If you see that it will go longer, please let us know at the earliest possible moment. Other ships use the Port of Houston and the port maintains a tight schedule." She moved toward the door. "If that's all…" She waved toward the door. "I'll see you out."

Detective Green practically snarled at Ysabel. "Oh no you don't. That's far from *all*. And you'll definitely want to bring in your legal staff for what I have to say."

"And what is that?" Jackson stepped between Detective Green and Ysabel, his voice dangerously low.

"That forklift driver who died last night, Stephan Kenig, was dead before he crashed. Someone shot him in the head."

Ysabel gasped.

Jackson remained stoic. "And this has *what* to do with me?"

Green pinned Jackson with a narrow-eyed stare. "We found a gun close by. My bet is that the ballistics will match with the bullet we found in the victim."

Ysabel frowned. The man who died was the criminal, not so much a victim, and Detective Green was now treating Jackson like he was the criminal. "Again, what does this have to do with Mr. Champion?"

"Please, get to the point," Jackson said, his voice sharp, his fingers tightening into a fist.

"The point is," Detective Brody's mouth turned up in a smirk, "we ran a scan on the serial number. The SIG SAUER registration is in the name of Jackson Champion. Mr. Champion, we need you to come with us to the sheriff's office. We'll need fingerprints to match with those we found on the gun."

"I don't know what's going on here, but I didn't shoot

that man. I was chasing him because I thought he was stealing my saddles."

Green snorted. "Nevertheless, your gun appears to be the one that killed him."

"Detective." Tom Walker stood in the open doorway. "I was with Mr. Jackson during the chase. I can vouch for him. He didn't have a gun and he didn't shoot the other forklift driver."

Green didn't look happy to hear Tom's admission. "Are you willing to sign a statement to that effect?"

Tom's shoulders straightened until he looked as though he was a soldier standing at attention. "Absolutely."

"You'll have to come to headquarters, as well. I'll need a sworn statement from both you and Champion."

Jackson nodded toward Ysabel. "Call my attorney and meet me there."

Ysabel nodded as Detective Green slammed cuffs onto Jackson's wrists.

Jackson's jaw tightened, but he didn't wince.

Anger surged inside Ysabel at the rough treatment. "Is that necessary? Mr. Walker just told you Mr. Champion didn't do it. I'm sure he won't try to run from the law for something he isn't guilty of."

The detective snapped the cuffs shut. "Procedure."

Agent Fielding shook his head. "I don't think that's necessary."

"This is a local issue. If you have a problem with the way I handle it, take it up with my supervisor." Green shoved Jackson through the door.

Ysabel could have sworn Detective Green smiled as he led Jackson through the bay of offices, past Champion Shipping employees, treating Jackson like a common criminal.

Ysabel ran to her office, snatching up her BlackBerry and purse. "Come on, Tom, let's get there."

The elevator Jackson and the lawmen got into closed before she could get on. She jammed her finger on the down button, her toe tapping against the granite tiles while she waited for another car and someone to answer her call to the corporate law firm.

"Halston, Young and Franklin Law Firm, how may I help you?" a perky secretary said into her ear as the elevator door dinged open.

"This is Ysabel Sanchez with Champion Shipping. Mr. Jackson requests the immediate presence of Mr. Young at the sheriff's office. Let me stress, Mr. Young needs to be there ASAP."

"I CAN'T believe Detective Green dragged you into the station." Flint McKade paced the floor of his spacious office, his cowboy boots tapping against the wood flooring.

Jackson rubbed the back of his neck, tension pulling at the muscles there. "Yeah, he seemed to get a big kick out of parading me through the office in cuffs. My employees will get a good laugh at that." He shrugged, unfazed by the memory of his startled employees. Ysabel would give them the straight scoop. "Thank goodness I had a witness riding on the back of my forklift or I'd have been at the sheriff's office a lot longer than the two hours it took my lawyer to straighten out the mess." Jackson turned toward the door to the office. Where had Ysabel disappeared to? "What I'm pissed about is that someone broke into my home and stole my gun."

"I thought you had a brand-new security system installed last year?" Akeem Abdul leaned against the wood-paneled walls, his boots crossed at the ankle, looking laid back except for the intensity in his dark eyes. If not for the jeans, boots and denim shirt, he'd appear the most ferocious sheik in any desert—fierce and loyal to his friends.

"I did. I used the firm Deke recommended. They installed a state-of-the-art system. No one should have been able to enter without detection." His friend from college days at Texas A&M, Deke Norton, had promised him no one could penetrate the system without his explicit permission. Jackson smacked his hat against his leg. "I've got a call into Deke's security specialist to review the entire system."

Flint stopped in mid-pace. "What is Homeland Security saying?"

"The FBI agent in charge made noises that the detonators, the plane explosion, the man going overboard on my ship and the radioactive traces you found here at the ranch are making it look bad for the Aggie Four Foundation. They'll be poking around all of us with questions soon."

Flint nodded. "That explains the call I had from your man Fielding this morning. He wants to meet with me this afternoon. He'll be working the angle of the radiation-contaminated parts they found in the horse blankets smuggled with that last shipment of Arabians out of the Middle East. It's been three months and they still haven't pinned who brought in those parts. They suspect it's the rebel faction that staged the coup in Rasnovia, but they have no firm proof."

"Gentlemen, the evidence is looking bad for us." Jackson slapped his hat against his jeans again, frustration making him wish he could punch something or someone. "For me in particular, since my shipping business is the one bringing in the bad goods."

"You're not in this alone." Akeem pushed away from the wall, strode across the floor and held out a hand to Jackson.

Jackson clasped it with both hands. "Thanks."

"That's right," Flint said, closing the distance and covering their joined hands with his own. "The Aggie Four is a team and we'll see this thing through."

"This is reassuring." Ysabel walked in carrying a tray of

iced tea Flint's cook, Lucinda, had prepared. "Have you figured out how to keep our man Jackson out of jail?"

Akeem reached for the tea, "Nah, we thought we'd let him rot there, while we spend his fortune."

"Yeah," Flint grinned. "The man has more than enough to share."

Ysabel rolled her eyes. "Like you two don't? Give me a break. No, really, what are you planning?"

Flint abandoned his smile, deep furrows etched across his forehead. "We plan a thorough search into our employee databases for answers to who's behind the smuggling."

"You two have had dealings with Detective Green before, haven't you?" Ysabel asked.

Akeem nodded. "Sure, he was on the case when Flint's sister Taylor's son, Christopher, was kidnapped."

"Yeah and he was there to investigate the explosion and shootings on the airplane that took the lives of three of my men," Flint added.

Jackson twisted the brim of his cowboy hat. "I don't trust the man."

"Any reason in particular?" Akeem asked.

"He seemed more than happy to jump on any excuse to bust me."

"I noticed that." Ysabel set her tea glass on a coaster. "It was as though he enjoyed seeing you booked and finger-printed. He was outright angry when Tom's sworn statement kept you from occupying a jail cell."

"Do you still have connections inside the sheriff's office?" Akeem asked.

Jackson nodded to Ysabel. "That would be Ysabel's connection. One of your cousins, right?"

"Mitch Stanford. He's married to my cousin Rosa." Ysabel retrieved her BlackBerry from her purse and scanned the contact names until she found Mitch. "I'll give him a call and ask him to keep an eye open for anything that might surface concerning the case."

"Thanks." Jackson stared down at his Stetson, lost in thought. "Why are these things happening to us?"

"It's as if someone has it in for the Aggie Four Foundation, maybe us in particular," Akeem said, as he gazed out the window at the acres of lush green pastures.

"You think they had anything to do with Viktor's death?" Flint paused to stare at a picture hanging on the wall of the four of them when they were in college, arms linked over their shoulders, all wearing swim trunks on South Padre beach. The senior trip they'd scrimped and saved their hard-earned money for.

Jackson had a copy on his desk in his office. The Aggie Four had been there for him since they'd all vowed to become billionaires back in their college days. And damned if they didn't all make it.

"Viktor's death was half a world away in Rasnovia," Ysabel observed, her hand poised over the BlackBerry.

Her voice jerked Jackson out of his thoughts, his head snapped up and he stared across at her. A raw, festering ache reverberated through his body at the sight of her. Ysabel had tendered her resignation.

Yet she sat on the leather, wingback chair, her slim knees crossed, long gorgeous legs tipped in sexy black heels. She could wear a brown paper bag and still make a man's blood boil.

He pulled his gaze from those legs and forced his mind away from how they'd wrapped around his waist and how she'd cried out his name in lust-filled passion. No, now wasn't the time to get a rise or worry about how he could keep his prized executive assistant.

"That's true. Viktor and his family were murdered in Rasnovia." Jackson's chest tightened, but he forced himself to move on. "The smuggling also *began* half a world away. The shipment with the saddles and detonators originated in Rasnovia."

Akeem perched on the edge of Flint's desk. "I'm amazed you were able to ship anything out of Rasnovia with a civil war ravaging the country since the royal family's death."

"Given what the police found in that box, I'm beginning to think it's not so amazing." Jackson captured Ysabel's gaze. "Have you heard anything on that database scan of employees?"

"Not yet. I have Tom working it."

"You sure he's the man for the job? He's so new to the company."

"If you'd read his résumé, you'd have noticed he won numerous awards for breaking into supposedly air-tight computer security systems. He knows his way around a computer."

Jackson shook his head and stared at her as if she'd lost her mind. "You hired a hacker?"

"He's only a hacker in a good way. Pinkerton confirmed his background check. Besides, I liked him."

A surge of something akin to anger pushed through Jackson, making him want to lash out at the young guy Ysabel had hired. "You trust him inside Champion Shipping's computer systems?"

"Absolutely." She crossed her arms over her chest, the stubborn tilt to her chin one he'd seen before when she'd fought for a point in which she believed.

Flint grinned at the exchange. "You know Ysabel's instincts have paid off for you in more instances than you can count. You better keep her on the payroll."

Akeem chuckled. "Yeah, I'd hate to see her go to work for the competition."

Their seemingly innocuous comments hit Jackson square in the gut. What they didn't know was that Ysabel had more or less given her two-week notice. Although the noncompete clause in her contract would keep her from going to work for his competitors, she wouldn't be working for him anymore. And that's what he didn't want to think about or acknowledge.

"What about the road-rage incident last night?" Ysabel reminded him. "If someone has it in for you all, wouldn't they try to run the rest of you off the road, as well?"

Akeem nodded. "Sadly, when you've clawed your way to the top like we have, you accumulate enemies along the way. Some even out to cause us trouble for the cash."

"Christopher's kidnapping." Ysabel's hand rose to cover her stomach, making Jackson think she might be having a relapse of yesterday's sickness. Instinctively, he moved forward several steps before he stopped himself. She'd be ticked if he hovered over her like he had yesterday. But that couldn't stop him from keeping a close eye on her.

"What got me about that whole kidnapping scare was that the police seemed to know what was going to happen almost before it did," Flint said.

"Like how did they know where the kidnappers were taking the boy almost before Taylor and I got there?" Akeem asked.

"An insider leaking it out," Flint stated. It was his nephew who'd been in danger, his sister who'd gone after him with only Akeem to protect her. Akeem had been there for her. Both Flint and Jackson would trust the Texas sheik with their own lives and had on more than one occasion.

Jackson shook his head. "More like an insider giving the orders." He shot a look toward Ysabel.

"I'm on it boss. I'll let my cousin know to keep a look out for a dirty cop while I'm asking him to keep us posted on the investigation."

"*Señor* McKade?" Lucinda appeared at the door.

Flint nodded toward the housekeeper/cook. "Yes, what is it?"

"*Señor* Norton is here to see you."

"Deke?" Flint's brows tugged inward. "I don't remember scheduling a meeting with Deke." He shrugged. "Send him in. Maybe he can shed some light on this mess."

Jackson raised a hand. "I'd rather not mention it yet. I want to find out more before we share inside information outside this room. If word gets out to the press that Champion Shipping and the Aggie Four Foundation are involved in international terrorism, we could be ruined."

"And you don't want our financial adviser to know this." Flint nodded. "Gotcha." He tipped his head to Lucinda. "Show him in."

"Sí, señor." She backed out of the doorway and hurried away.

"Not that I don't trust Deke, but he is a financial adviser after all. I don't want to put him in the position of knowing something about the market before it happens." Jackson stared around the room at each of the individuals there. "Because of his friendship with all of us it could be considered insider trading."

A moment later, Deke Norton opened the door and strode in. "Did you see the news?" He walked across to the flat-screen, plasma television set hanging on the wall over the fireplace and pressed the power button.

"Why?" Jackson hadn't had time to watch the news between running his corporation, spending two hours at the Harris County Sheriff's Office and then heading out to the Diamondback Ranch to meet with the Aggie Four. Who had time to watch the news when your world was crumbling around you?

"You'll want to see this." Deke nodded toward the screen.

A local Houston news anchor blinked into focus. "Late breaking news." He glanced down at a sheet of paper in his hand. "Houston shipping mogul and former most eligible Texas bachelor, Jackson Champion, was taken into custody today as a possible suspect in the murder of a forklift driver last night at the Port of Houston."

"Damn." Jackson slapped his Stetson against his knee.

"Shh!" Deke turned up the volume. "It gets worse."

"Preliminary investigations indicate that he may have shot the man to silence him after the forklift driver discovered a smuggled shipment of detonators coming off a Champion Shipping cargo ship. Houston police detectives, the sheriff's office and Homeland Security are scrambling to find out just how bad the threat is." The reporter stared into the camera. "The shipping giant who already owns half of Houston, is under FBI, Houston P.D. and Homeland Security scrutiny."

Akeem shook his fist at the screen. "Where did they get that crap?"

"Here we go again," Flint punched the Power button, switching the television off. "The press making a mockery out of our judicial system. Since when were they elected judge, jury and executioner? Makes you sound guilty without all the evidence."

"How did they get that information?" Akeem asked. "It's not public knowledge, is it?"

"Only an insider in the investigation would have that information to peddle." Once again Jackson's gaze shot to Ysabel.

She opened her mouth to tell him she'd ask her cousin José, who worked at that particular television station, to get with her cousin at the sheriff's department to find out who the anchor's source was. A glance at Deke made her close her lips and rethink her words. "I'll get on it."

"Let me guess…" Akeem shook his head, smiling. "Another cousin?"

Flint asked, "How many cousins do you have, Ysabel?"

She stood, digging her cell phone out of her purse. "Too many to count." Most of her family and extended family lived in the Houston area. She'd hate to leave them to start over by herself.

Once outside Flint's office, Ysabel breathed a sigh of relief. Torn between wanting to know what was going on and wanting to be as far away from Jackson as possible, she felt as though her insides were tied in knots. She worked her way back to the kitchen where Lucinda was preparing a light snack for the men.

Lucinda handed her dry saltines. "Take these. They will help settle your stomach."

"Why do you think I need them?"

"It happens to most women during the early months. The nausea, the upset tummy."

Ysabel stared down at her belly. "How did you—"

"Know you are with child?" Lucinda laughed and lifted the tray. "I could see it in your face, in the way you hold your hand over *la niña* and the way you stare at *Señor* Jackson." She patted Ysabel's belly. "She will be beautiful like her mama and papa."

Ysabel dropped into a chair, the crackers clutched in her hand. If Lucinda could tell just by looking at her, what was to keep Jackson from knowing?

She dragged in a deep breath and fought back the tears so ready to fall at just about anything. Shoving a cracker in her mouth, she focused on keeping it down while she thumbed through her BlackBerry for her cousins' numbers. This smuggling stuff had to resolve quickly so that she could get on with her life and away from Jackson.

Chapter Five

"Mr. Champion, I think I've found something." Tom Walker jumped up from his desk and followed Jackson into his office. The staff had left for the day, except for the young manager trainee.

Ysabel had insisted on stopping at her apartment on their way back from the Diamondback Ranch, something about a date with her sister.

How could she consider a date with her sister more important than what was happening to Champion Shipping? And although she'd insisted they needed to talk the night before, she'd done anything but talk on the way back from the ranch.

She'd spoken less than ten words the entire hour and a half it took them to get back to Houston in rush-hour traffic. Jackson didn't like it. He'd rather she ranted and raved like any self-respecting woman angry at not getting her way. At least then he might get a clue as to what was going on in her convoluted head.

But she'd sat in the passenger seat of his pickup, her hands folded in her lap, her focus on the windshield, not him. He'd tried several times to start a conversation. He'd asked about the cousins she'd called, she'd answered in monosyllables. Gone was her willingness to exchange ideas with him, to argue about politics and condemn his lack of a personal life.

By the time they'd reached Houston, he was so frustrated he'd wanted to grab her by the shoulders and shake her out of the silent treatment.

But she'd flung the truck door open and jumped out before he could stop her. Damned woman!

"Sir? Did you want to hear what I found?" Tom repeated.

"Yes, yes, of course." Jackson turned toward the eager young man, much like himself at the tender age of twenty-two. "What did you find?"

"I did a scan on all employees hired in the past six months, both here in Houston and also in several of your Middle Eastern locations, as well as those in Rasnovia."

Jackson's spirits improved slightly, his attention firmly rooted on the trainee. "And?"

"I pulled up the employee photographs of twenty people and sent them to Miss Sanchez's cousin at the Harris County Sheriff's Office and he ran it through a database of persons of interest." Tom smiled. "We got a hit on four of the men. One of them was the forklift driver, Stephan Kenig. They match up with a group the CIA have been tracking who've been spotted in a Syrian terrorist training camp in the past year." The young man handed him a computer printout with employee personal data and the pictures of the men.

Jackson glanced at the names and shook his head, amazed at the amount of information the guy had accumulated in such a short time. "Her cousin told you all that?"

Tom shrugged. "I've been on the computer and phone most of the day passing information. But it was Miss Sanchez who called and told me what her cousin found out. She wanted me to tell you that she was on her way back to the office and should be here in about…" Tom glanced down at his watch and looked outside Jackson's door. "Now." He grinned and stepped out of the doorway.

Ysabel walked into the office. Gone was her profession-ally tailored skirt suit. In its place was a pair of faded blue jeans and an oversize sweatshirt, the neckline torn out and hanging over one shoulder like an eighties dance queen. She looked young and vulnerable, more like a teen from the barrio than a high-powered executive assistant. She dumped her purse in a chair and pushed her sleeves up past her elbows. "Did you look up the address on the man here in Houston?"

"Got it." Tom handed her a sheet of paper. "Greg Voleski, aka Gregor Volsky."

"Have you passed the addresses on to my cousin at the sheriff's office yet?" she asked.

The young man handed her a copy of the papers he'd given to Jackson. "I was just about to hit send on the e-mail when Mr. Champion showed up."

Ysabel pressed her lips together. "Send it and then go home for the evening. You've done more than enough for the day."

"But if there's anything else I can do…" Tom stared from Jackson to Ysabel, his gaze stopping with Ysabel as though she was the boss, not Jackson.

Jackson fought the smile threatening to break through. Ysabel ran the corporation as well as he did. Sometimes better. And his employees respected her abilities and intelligence.

Ysabel smiled at the trainee. "Get some rest. I need you sharp for whatever comes up tomorrow. Now get that info to my cousin, pronto!"

Tom darted through the door.

Jackson crossed the floor, closed and locked the door behind Tom. "He's going to make a hell of a good employee."

"I know." Ysabel moved a step away from Jackson and stared down at the paper in her hand. "I know where this apartment building is. It's near to where I grew up in my old neighborhood."

Jackson leaned over her shoulder to look at the address. "If he even thought there was a chance the law was onto him, he'd be long gone."

Ysabel's eyes narrowed. "Then let's get there before he has the chance."

"No way. The man's a trained terrorist." Jackson tried to take the paper from her.

She jerked her hand back, but not before his fingers closed on the sheet. She held tight. "Like you said, he's probably long gone. What would it hurt to go check out his place and see if there's anything that would help us in our investigation?"

"Ysabel." Jackson didn't like where she was leading. "Let the police handle it."

She refused to release the paper, staging a mini tug-of-war with him. "The Aggie Four agreed to the idea that there is someone crooked on the police force or in the sheriff's office. Are you going to trust them to do it right?"

She had a point. And she wasn't giving up the paper. If he didn't agree to go with her to this man's apartment, he wouldn't put it past her to go on her own. Fear pinched his chest, an image of the dead forklift driver's charred remains firmly rooted in his memory. "Okay. You've convinced me. Give me the paper and *I'll* go." He tugged on the paper, determined to get it from her. Instead, he ended up ripping it in half.

She retained the half with the address on it, holding it up behind her, out of his reach. "I'm going with you."

"If you weren't already quitting, I'd fire you on the spot for insubordination." He reached over her shoulder, grabbing the scrap of paper. Their fingers connected, a charge of electricity exploding through his nerve endings like gasoline in a combustion engine.

She held on, refusing to let him have the address. The result was to bring him closer to her than they'd been since *The Night*. The exotic scent of her hair wafted up to assault his senses, the warmth of her skin teasing him with its nearness.

"Go ahead," she said, her voice but a whisper as if she couldn't quite catch her breath. "If you remember, I wanted to resign, but you had to throw an employment contract at me like a prenup agreement in a divorce case." Her gaze dropped from his eyes to his mouth, her breathing becoming more shallow and erratic. She wasn't immune to him like she'd led him to believe with her silent treatment and aloof behavior.

"I need you Ysabel." *More than I ever thought possible.* But he had to keep it on the professional level. "And you owe me a two-week notice."

Ysabel's eyelids drooped to half mast and she swayed toward Jackson. "Does everything have to be on your terms and your terms only?" Her words had dropped to a murmur, as if she couldn't get enough air into or out of her lungs.

"Damn right." She had him tied in a knot so tight he couldn't remember how to breathe either. He let her have the paper, his hand curling around the back of her neck feathering through the silky smooth hair falling down to her waist.

"Someone needs to teach you a lesson on compromise." Her own arms twined around his neck and she brought his mouth exquisitely closer to hers.

He stopped a breath away from her lips. "And I know just the one who can do it." Then his lips closed over hers, his other hand circling her waist, drawing her soft body against his harder one.

Two months hadn't been nearly long enough to erase Ysabel from his mind, hadn't been long enough to make him forget how she felt against him, the taste of her lips, the warmth of her hands on his skin.

His body remembered, his mind rejoiced and he fell into

her like a dehydrated man fell into an oasis pool, lapping up the very essence of her.

Her mouth opened on a moan and his tongue delved in, twisting and toying with hers. She tasted of mint and chocolate, the sweetness wrapping around him, drawing him deeper into her.

When her head dropped back, he stole the opportunity to lavish kisses along the smooth line of her throat, nipping at the vein pumping madly beneath the skin.

She tugged at his shirt, pulling it from the waistband of his jeans so that she could slide her hands beneath it. Long, tapered fingers climbed up his taut abs, skimming over his ribs to rest against the muscles of his chest.

His fingers slipped beneath the sweatshirt hanging loosely from her shoulders, finding the gentle curve of her waist, the silky skin feverish to his touch. His hands climbed ever upward until his palms cupped the swell of her breasts.

She had beautiful breasts, full and lush, tipped with the prettiest rosy-brown nipples a man could ever want.

His mouth watered with the need to taste them. He grabbed the hem of the sweatshirt and ripped it up over her head, tossing it to the floor.

She flicked the buttons of his shirt, loosening them one at a time, until he thought he might come undone if she didn't finish in the next two seconds. Before she could release the bottom two buttons, he saved her the effort, ripping them apart.

Then he pulled her to him, her lace-covered breasts tangling in the hairs on his chest, teasing his senses with the wispy scrap of material. He reached behind her and flicked the hooks. Then he slid the straps over her shoulders…slowly…his gaze drinking in the way she spilled into his palms.

The hard ridge beneath his trousers tightened painfully.

When her hand reached between them and stroked him,

he gasped. He'd dreamed of this every night for the past two months, his sleep disturbed with images of Ysabel standing before him naked.

Now she was here, naked from the waist up. As if driven by the demons of his nightmares, he reached out and unbuttoned her jeans, tugging the zipper down until he could see the lacy black panties beneath. The slight swell of her belly complimented her full hips and made him want more. She wasn't model-thin like many of his previous women. Not Ysabel. Her Hispanic heritage gave her curves in all the best places.

He dropped to one knee and kissed her belly button.

She raised a hand and brushed it across his cheek, a sad kind of shadow crossing her eyes.

"Do you want me to stop?" he asked, unsure whether he could at this point.

She shook her head and pulled his head to her belly, where he pressed his lips, tonguing her belly button.

Clutching the edges of her waistband, Jackson tugged the jeans downward, trailing kisses across her belly button and down to the thin elastic of her panties. He hooked his thumbs beneath the elastic surrounding her thighs and stroked the fine, curly hairs beneath, rubbing over the sweet spot that made her crazy.

She cried out, her hips pressing closer.

With his body straining to hold back, Jackson jerked the jeans and panties the rest of the way down. The past two months fell away and Jackson was back in the heaven of Ysabel's arms.

She slipped out of her shoes and clothes, standing before him in nothing but skin. Tingling, sensitized skin that yearned to feel his skin against it.

"You're so beautiful." His hands slid up the backs of her calves and he pressed a kiss to her kneecaps. "Stubborn, sexy, beautiful Ysabel."

His words made her melt inside. She wanted to believe she meant something more to him than any of the other women he'd paraded past her over the years. If he even gave her a hint that this would go beyond another one-night stand, she'd blurt out that she'd fallen in love with him the day she'd interviewed for the job as his executive assistant.

That was the problem. She knew his track record. Knew the name of each woman he'd taken to bed since she'd come to work for him. Knew what happened afterward, how he stopped calling, stopped dating and eventually forgot about them.

Knowing all that, why didn't she stop him?

Because she wanted him so intensely, she'd risk a broken heart for one last time with him.

His thumbs massaged her inner thighs. It felt so good, her knees fell open as if they knew what to do even if Ysabel couldn't make sense of her chaotic thoughts.

Jackson's fingers parted her folds and he took her in his mouth, tonguing her until she thought she would explode into a zillion little pieces if he didn't quit.

She pulled away, her breathing ragged, coming in short, rapid gasps. The need for oxygen came secondary to the other kind of need pulsing through her, making her wild with desire.

Jackson rose in front of her. Hooking his elbows beneath her knees, he lifted her into his arms.

Ysabel wrapped her legs around him, settling over the bulge in his trousers, wishing he were as naked as she was, feeling very much the seductress, naked and wanton in the CEO's office. Instead of shocking her and making her cringe with guilt and shame, it empowered her. She'd brought him to this point. He desired her, even if he could never love her.

He carried her across the carpeted office and settled her bottom on the cool, slick surface of his desk.

Before he could change his mind, she reached for him, making quick work of his belt, button and fly. She wanted him inside her, filling that place that had been empty since the day he'd left her alone in his apartment.

His jeans slipped to his ankles, caught on his boots, his boxer shorts quickly followed.

She took him in her hands, loving the sexy feel of silk on steel. Gently, slowly, greedily, she guided him to her, pressing him against her opening.

Jackson paused, sucked in a shaky breath and let it out slowly. "We weren't careful before, we shouldn't risk it a second time. I have protection in my wallet."

"Don't worry," she said, clasping his buttocks in her palms she guided him home, his shaft filling and stretching her deliciously moist channel. He was so hard, warm and sexy, she couldn't wait.

Fully encased inside her, his muscles straining against her fingers, Jackson froze. "Are you sure? I could pull out at the last second?"

Rocking against him, in the age-old rhythm of mating, Ysabel couldn't take his reticence much longer. She wanted it all and she wanted it now. "No. Really. It's already taken care of. I can't get pregnant." At the back of her lust-filled mind, she almost laughed hysterically. Nice of him to worry now, when it was way past too late. She couldn't get pregnant because she already was.

He grasped her face between his hands and kissed her with such tenderness, she thought she would die. "We still need to talk," he said, smoothing a stray tear from her cheek.

"Later." She leaned back, bracing her hands in the middle of his desk, her breasts thrusting toward the ceiling, her hair feathering across her back.

His hands on her hips, Jackson's thrusts built a delicious friction inside her, heating her core to the point of meltdown.

As the thrusts increased in tempo, tension built inside her until she felt as taut as a cocked bow. Then she shot over the edge, hurtling into the most intense sensations she'd only experienced one other time in her life. The first and only other night she and Jackson made love. The night they'd made the baby growing in her belly.

Jackson clutched her tightly against him, filling her to full and held her steady as he emptied his seed into her.

Ysabel's legs dropped down and she wrapped her arms around him, hiding her face against his chest, tears wetting her cheeks. All too soon, she'd leave. Jackson would forget about her and she'd only have memories of this night together. Memories and a baby to love.

"What's this?" He tipped her head back and brushed a thumb beneath her eye.

"Nothing."

"Did I hurt you?"

"No." *But you will.* She pushed him away and dropped to her feet, her cheeks burning, guilt raging through her. He had the right to know about his baby. But she couldn't tell him now. The urge to run hit her like a panic attack. "I just have to go."

"But we need to talk."

"No, we don't." She grabbed for her jeans, her legs shaking so hard, it took her several attempts to get them in the pant legs and pull up. Tossing the sweatshirt over her head, she yanked it down over her naked breasts and ran for the door.

Jackson's hand caught her before she turned the handle. "Stop. We can't leave things like this." His brows dipped downward, his blue eyes strangely sad and pensive.

Now wasn't the time to feel bad about leaving Jackson. If she didn't do it now, she'd only feel worse when he dumped her later. "We shouldn't have done this. It only complicates the situation."

"Damn it, Ysabel!" he exploded. "Having you in my life complicates everything."

She stared up at him for a moment, then her gaze dropped to her bare feet. "Yeah. But not much longer. You have to put up with me for only thirteen more days, then I'll be out of your life for good." She jerked loose of his hold and dived for the door. If she didn't get out, she'd dissolve into a weeping mess at his feet.

"Ysabel!" he yelled after her.

She glanced back to see him scrambling for his clothing.

With a head start, she'd make it to the elevator before him. In a mad dash she raced for the elevator bay.

Relief washed over her when she spied the open elevator. She dashed in and punched the lobby level. The door closed, ever so slowly.

"Ysabel, wait!"

Jackson ran toward the elevator, pushing his arm through a sleeve as he raced across the granite tile, skidding to a stop just as the door closed completely. As the elevator jerked and silently descended toward the ground, fists pounded on the metal door above. "Ysabel! Damn it! This is crazy. I know where you live!"

Ysabel stared up at the ceiling of the elevator car, fully expecting Jackson to break through it and shake the truth out of her. When he didn't, she leaned against the mirrored wall and slid to the floor, her tears drying.

She'd only managed to delay the inevitable and piss off Jackson at the same time. She had to come to work the next day or risk being sued for every cent she owned, and right now, she needed all the money she could find to help her through the next few months of job hunting and settling in a new town. No, she couldn't avoid him, but she needed breathing space, if only for the remainder of the night.

Going back to her apartment right away wasn't an option.

He'd be sure to show up there and demand an explanation she wasn't prepared to give.

She'd left the address of the other suspect in his office, forgotten in her desperate attempt to recapture something she'd never had in the first place. Ysabel closed her eyes and visualized the paper Tom had given her. Her photographic memory kicked in and numbers and letters appeared in her mind. She remembered.

Too distraught to go home, she might as well check out the apartment where Greg Voleski lived. She didn't know what she'd do once she got there, but she had to do something, rather than wait around for Jackson to show up and expose her secret. The fireworks in that situation were sure to be devastating. What could be worse at Greg's apartment?

Chapter Six

When Jackson reached the parking garage, Ysabel's taillights blinked at him, rounding the corner to the exit, mocking his attempt to catch up with her. He made a mental note to talk with the elevator maintenance man. No elevator should be that incredibly slow.

He ran for his truck, throwing himself inside. She'd be out of the garage before he could catch her and even at night there would be enough traffic in downtown Houston he'd have a hell of a time following her.

So he had to outthink her. Where would Ysabel go?

If she were smart, she'd go straight home and wait for Jackson to catch up to her and shake some sense into her head. But then Ysabel was a woman and she didn't think like him—a mere man.

Jackson pulled out onto the street and looked both ways. No sign of Ysabel's bright red compact car, only lights from other people hurrying home after a late day at the office. Why couldn't they have gone home earlier like normal people?

Jackson chuckled. Because they were like *him*. Driven by some force, whether it was the almighty dollar, an unreasonable deadline or an evil boss bent on ruining their social lives, the people leaving downtown late were much like he'd been two months ago. Compelled to work his life away, all his efforts concentrated on increasing his already-massive fortune. When had becoming a billionaire become an obsession? When was enough enough?

Jackson's truck idled as he pondered which direction to take—his current predicament a metaphor of his life.

At an early age, he'd vowed never to be poor again. He and his college buddies, the Aggie Four, made a pact to become billionaires and they had. Now what?

Now he found himself defending his corporation and his friends from a vicious attack, one that could ruin them, and all he could think about was Ysabel and the screwed up way he'd handled their relationship. Never mind he could go to jail and lose everything he'd worked so hard to attain. Never mind someone was out, possibly to kill him. He couldn't leave things the way they were between himself and his executive assistant. Hell, he'd already violated one of his self-imposed cardinal rules: Don't get involved with your employees. Maybe she was right by resigning.

His gut tightened. To hell with her being right. She couldn't quit. He needed her.

Jackson slammed his palm against the steering wheel. "Where the hell did you go, Ysabel Sanchez?" he shouted to his windshield.

Think, Jackson. Think like a female. Think like Ysabel.

She'd expect him to show up at her apartment. Hadn't he shouted he knew where she lived? Yeah, she'd think he'd go there first. Therefore, she'd avoid going there until later.

Her sister's apartment? Jackson glanced at the clock on his dash. Already past ten o'clock at night, she wouldn't bother her sister this late. Would she? Jackson had been there on one occasion when he'd dropped off Ysabel after a trip to New York City. He could probably figure out where it was again. But was that where she'd be?

Then he remembered what they'd been fighting over when he'd lost his mind and kissed her. She'd insisted on coming with him to Greg Voleski's apartment.

When he'd been gathering his clothes off the floor of his office, Jackson had shoved the scrap of paper into his pocket and grabbed the papers Tom had given him with the other two men's names. He reached for the torn paper now and studied the address. Would Ysabel remember it? With her superb memory, probably. Would she be stupid enough to go there at night in a neighborhood of questionable safety?

Hell, yes! Rather than go home and risk running into him, she'd place herself in a dangerous situation. She didn't have the address with her and would assume Jackson would think she'd forget. And she was just stubborn enough to go alone to a place that hadn't been safe even when she'd been growing up there.

Jackson switched on the GPS unit in the dash of his truck and keyed in the address. Once on the road to the apartment building in southwest Houston, he tapped the speed dial number for Akeem on the hands-free cell phone device also built into the dash of his customized pickup.

Akeem answered on the first ring, his voice coming over the speaker phone loud and clear. "Hey, Jackson. What do you know?"

"I need you to use your connections in Rasnovia to find two men who were on Champion Shipping's payroll." He filled in Akeem on what Tom and Ysabel's cousin at the sheriff's office had learned and the names of the two men.

"I'll get right on it. Hey, Jackson, I've been thinking about it, you might consider beefing up your personal security. I know you don't like the idea of a bodyguard, but with one attempt on your life already, it might be time to break down and get one."

Jackson had rejected what must have been hundreds of

sales calls from personal protection agencies. Since his name came out in the Houston newspaper as one of the most eligible bachelors in the state of Texas, listing a rough accounting of his assets, he'd been getting nonstop phone calls. It was enough to bring out not only every gold digger this side of the Mississippi, but others from around the world.

The article had brought out the weirdos, solicitors and every charity wanting a piece of Champion Shipping assets. Ysabel had managed to run interference, deflecting even the most insistent. Jackson didn't have the patience. However, he'd turned to his friend Deke Norton for advice on installing new security systems in all of his residences and offices. He still wanted to handle his personal security on his own, primarily by keeping a low profile when out and dressing like any other Texan, in discount store jeans and cowboy boots. Besides, they were more comfortable.

"Thanks, Akeem. I'll think about it." He clicked the Off button as he turned off the main road into a Southside neighborhood where streetlights illuminated the peeling paint and general state of disrepair common among low-rent properties managed by slum lords or subsidized by the government.

Young men, wearing the ultra-baggy shorts whose crotches hung down below their knees, loitered in groups against the sides of buildings, the tips of their cigarettes glowing bright red in the shadows. Chains hung from their belt loops to their pockets, the shiny silver glinting in the light from the corner streetlight.

Jackson reached beneath his seat for the handgun he kept close by, his own personal bodyguard, in his opinion.

As he waited at a stoplight for the red to change to green, he took in the ominous air of the neighborhood. He'd thought he had it bad growing up in foster homes. However, this neighborhood had him beat. He couldn't imagine a kid of his walking alone or in a group down one of these streets.

He tried to convince himself that it couldn't be as bad as he was making it. Lots of people lived here, young and old. But the reports of drive-by shootings always came out of these poorer, more desperate living conditions.

A cold wave of dread washed over him. Ysabel was out here somewhere if she really did come to investigate Voleski's apartment. Jackson hoped like hell she'd gone to her sister's instead.

The GPS unit led him deeper into the community until he rounded a corner and the three-story apartment building appeared filling the block to his right.

He pulled into the parking area, his shiny new truck a glaring contrast to the dilapidated vehicles lined up on the broken pavement. At the end of the parking lot, he spied a bright red compact car with rosary beads hanging from the rearview mirror and his stomach dropped. Ysabel.

Ysabel knew exactly where the apartment complex was. She remembered hurrying by it when she was a young girl on her way to the neighborhood elementary school. One of the teenagers who babysat her on occasion had told her a woman had been found strangled to death in one of the apartments. From that time on, Ysabel got a severe case of the creeps passing by the building. She'd even walk two blocks out of her way to avoid the area altogether.

Her bright red car stood out as a new car, but the bangs and dents from the collision the night before made it fit in somewhat with the other dented vehicles in the parking lot. Still, to avoid drawing attention, she'd parked at the very end next to the Dumpster, hoping the smell of rotting garbage was enough of a deterrent to keep anyone from stealing the car or its various parts while she snooped around Gregor Volsky's apartment.

When she got out of her car, she'd begun to think maybe she'd made a huge mistake. A pregnant woman had no right to risk her own life, much less her baby's, by sneaking around a potential terrorist's apartment. Standing beside her car, she'd hesitated.

Hell, she was here already, what would it hurt to see if anyone was home? She didn't have to barge in or make her presence known.

Ysabel climbed the steps to the second floor and followed the concrete catwalk to apartment 212. Thankfully, the streetlight didn't shed much light from either end of the street, casting this particular apartment into the shadows.

The blinds were drawn and as far as Ysabel could tell, no lights were on inside.

"If you're looking for *Señor* Voleski, he moved out this morning."

Ysabel jumped, her heart slamming against her ribcage.

A small, leathery-skinned woman with thin, graying blond hair leaned against the open door of apartment number 213, her arms folded over her chest, a cigarette dangling from her lips.

Ysabel forced a smile, her stomach rebelling at the scent of burning tobacco. "I'm sorry, what did you say?"

The older woman's eyes narrowed. "You aren't one of his relatives, are you?"

"No, I'm not, why?"

"He gave me most of his stuff, said he wasn't coming back." Her eyes widened as though a thought had come to her. "You're not here to repossess his stuff or something, are you? Because if you are, he didn't give me nothin'." She stepped back into her apartment and hurried to close the door.

Ysabel stopped her by pressing a foot into the space, regretting her movement when the door crunched her toes into the doorframe. She winced, but didn't cry out. "Wait. I'm not here to collect anything. I just want to know where I can find Mr. Voleski."

"I don't know, he mumbled something about gettin' on some ship tonight and that he wouldn't be back to this rat hole ever again, or any other rat hole for that matter." She shrugged. "His words. Why are you looking for him? Is he in some kind of trouble?" She stared down at the foot preventing her from closing the door and then her glance rose to Ysabel. "Because if he is, I don't know *nada*." She removed the cigarette from her lips and blew smoke into Ysabel's face.

How she kept from launching the contents of her belly onto the blonde, Ysabel didn't know, but she did long enough to ask, "Can you tell me anything about him?" She waved a hand in front of her face to clear the smoke.

"No. I didn't talk to him much, he didn't talk to me at all. That's the way it is. Most people mind their own business."

"Did you overhear any odd noises coming from his apartment, ever see what he kept in there?"

"No. I mind my own business. I took a few things, but nothing worth much. I don't think he told the apartment manager he was leaving. Again, not my problem if he skips out on the rent. The door's not locked. He left like he wasn't ever coming back. Me and 215 helped ourselves. Not much left, but you're welcome to it."

Ysabel moved her foot. The woman had helped with more information than she would have thought to ask. Too bad she'd been through the man's belongings before Ysabel had a chance to look. "He didn't by chance have a computer or any electronics, did he?"

The door closed a little more. "Nothing you'd want. Just some busted clocks and radios." She shut the door before Ysabel could ask any more questions.

Ysabel returned to apartment number 212 and reached for the doorknob.

Something thwacked against the doorframe next to her head and splintered wood caught in her hair.

What the hell?

Ysabel ducked low, the wrought iron railing providing little barrier to whoever was throwing things at her. She peered up at the hole left in the wood. A small hole the size of a bullet showed up black against the dirty white of the faded paint. Crap! Someone wasn't throwing things; he was shooting at her!

She dropped to her belly hugging the concrete.

"Ysabel?" The voice coming from the stairwell made her heart leap.

"Jackson?" she whispered. "Jackson?" her voice growing in strength. As quickly as her relief flared to life, it plummeted. "Get down! Someone's shooting at me."

Instead of heeding her words, his footsteps pounded the rest of the way up the metal and concrete stairs. "Ysabel, get down!"

"I *am* down. *You* get down," she yelled back at him, afraid he'd burst into full view, giving the shooter a broad target to aim for.

Another bullet winged over the top of her head, close enough she felt the air whiff her hair. "Damn!" She couldn't believe it. She'd only stopped by to check things out. It wasn't as if she was going to try to make a citizen's arrest or anything. She was a woman, not some macho cop. A pregnant woman who had no business putting herself or her baby at risk.

Great. She was wasting time second-guessing and bemoaning her poor judgment instead of getting the heck out of there.

"Ysabel? Talk to me, sweetheart," Jackson whispered loud enough for her to hear him. "Are you all right?"

He'd called her sweetheart. Ysabel's eyes pooled and she reached up to brush aside the ready tears. Her hormones had made her entirely too weepy for an independent, self-assured single woman. "I'm fine, but if you get yourself shot, I'll kill you."

A soft chuckle warmed her insides and made her think that perhaps everything would be okay if she just kept her cool. Jackson would help her out of this mess. Although how he'd do that without getting shot himself, she couldn't fathom.

He couldn't get to her without making himself a target and she wasn't getting anywhere by playing dead. She squirmed an inch, mimicking the low crawling soldiers from the black-and-white war movies she'd watched with her father back when she was a little girl. Keeping her head and belly as close to the concrete as possible, she inched her way across the landing, thankful that she wasn't any farther along in her pregnancy. Low-crawling would be out in a month or two. Not that she planned to ever low-crawl again, if she could help it.

Another bullet pinged against the wrought iron railing.

"Damn, Ysabel!" Jackson swore. "I'm coming for you."

"*Madre de Dios!* Don't!"

"Then for heaven's sake, stay still. I'll be back."

"What do you mean, you'll be back?" When he didn't answer, she almost raised her head to look for him, before she remembered the shooter had nailed the wall just above her head in a previous shot fired. "Jackson?"

Had he backed down the stairwell to go find their shooter? Didn't he know he could get himself killed? "Damn him!" she grumbled, her heart lodging in her throat. "He doesn't have the sense God gave a gnat. He'll get himself killed and then he'll never know he was going to be a daddy."

Suddenly, her insistence to keep her pregnancy a secret seemed like an incredibly selfish act. Jackson had every right to know he was going to be a father. Maybe then he wouldn't be so stupid crazy and think he had to go tackle some insane shooter.

Those darned tears welled in her eyes, blinding her. She had to make it to that stairwell and stop him, but how could she see when she was crying like a blubbering baby? She squinched up her muscles and wiggled across the concrete another few inches, the coarseness grazing her palms and elbows. "Jackson Champion, you better not get yourself killed," she whispered, the tears falling in earnest now.

She'd almost made it to the stairwell when she realized the bullets had stopped slamming into the building around her. Except for the noise from cars passing on the streets around the building, she couldn't hear anything.

Then from the far corner of the building, an engine revved and tires squealed.

"Damn!" Jackson's voice shouted from somewhere in the parking lot below.

The vehicle sped away until all was quiet again. Too quiet.

"Jackson?" she called out, her voice shaking. For several long seconds, he didn't respond.

Then his voice sounded from the corner of the building where the vehicle had taken off from. "He's gone, Ysabel. You can come down."

"Jackson?" She rose to her knees and peered through the wrought iron railing. "Are you okay?"

"I'm fine, just pissed. He got away and I didn't even get the license plate."

"But you're okay?" She grasped the railing and strained to see him, her entire body shaking.

"Yes."

Ysabel stood on trembling legs and brushed the dirt off her hands. "Good, because I'm going to kill you."

"You'll have to come down here to do it then." His dark silhouette appeared below her and he smiled up at her, the lights from a first-floor apartment glinting off his teeth.

"I will, after I've checked out Gregor's apartment."

The teeth disappeared. "No way, Ysabel. You get down here, right now."

"Apparently, you can't tell me what to do anymore than I can tell you to stay away from a deranged shooter." She turned her back on him and strode for apartment number 212, anger fueling her pace.

Footsteps pounded on the concrete and steel steps. "Ysabel! Don't you dare—"

She grabbed the knob and flung the door open. "I dared."

He caught her around the waist before she could step across the threshold into the apartment and flung her out of the doorway and behind him. "Are you insane?"

"No, I'm informed. Now move aside." Although she spoke to him with that tone she reserved for employees overstepping the line, she was thrilled at the way he'd rushed to protect her. Not that it meant anything. He'd protect any one of his employees. That's just the way Jackson Champion worked. Rough around the edges, but his bark was definitely much worse than his bite and he really cared about the people working for him.

Ysabel knew that behind his corporate shark exterior was a man who needed love just like anyone else. Like her.

"What a mess." Jackson hovered in the doorway, looking in without moving forward.

"His neighbor said he'd moved out, but didn't take anything."

"Looks like he took a lot."

"That would be 213 and 215. He told them they could have what they wanted." She leaned up on her tiptoes and gazed over Jackson's shoulder. "Looks like that was just about everything but the trash." Dirty clothing, old pizza boxes and broken furniture were just a few of the items littering the filthy carpet. The musty smell of misuse, stale food and lack of simple hygiene wafted out to Ysabel, making her gag. She swallowed hard, determined to look for anything that would tell her what the man was planning.

Jackson looked inside and scanned the parking lot behind him. "Okay, we'll both go in, but only because I can't leave you standing out here for our friend to come back and use as target practice."

"So magnanimous of you." Ysabel sucked in a deep breath of semi-fresh air before she slid past him into the apartment. With a finger pressed beneath her nose to stave off the overwhelming stench, she looked around the apartment. "What exactly are we looking for?"

"You tell me." He touched a hand to the middle of her back as he stepped in behind her. "I just followed you here."

"You were supposed to go home and leave me alone." Warmth spread from where his hand rested on her. Despite her words, to the contrary, she was glad he'd followed her.

"*You* were supposed to go home and leave Gregor's apartment alone."

"Seems to me, we both have a problem taking orders." She liked their open banter, which had been a part of the boss–employee relationship from the first time they met in her interview. She was certain Jackson hired her because she gave as good as she got on sarcasm. It was almost like old times, before they'd committed the ultimate folly and slept together. If not for the baby growing in her belly, she might have been able to push aside her feelings for the man and get on with the business of being his executive assistant again, and nothing else.

The baby changed everything.

Ysabel stepped away from his touch. "I guess I expected to find bomb parts or something."

"I'm not seeing anything that even resembles bomb-making materials." Jackson nudged a lump of dirty clothes aside to look beneath. "Not that I'm sure what those are. But there aren't any pipes or gunpowder, fertilizer or electronics that might indicate a bomb factory." He ducked into the miniscule bedroom and adjoining bathroom and called out, "Maybe he took them with him?"

In the kitchen, Ysabel froze. "What did you say?"

Jackson emerged from the bedroom and stared across the room at Ysabel, his brows dipping low. "Which part, about the material or about his taking them with him?"

"Madre de Dios," Ysabel whispered, making the sign of the cross over her chest.

Jackson closed the distance between them and clutched her arms. "What?"

She stared up at him, her body going cold. "He told the neighbor he was leaving on a ship and not coming back."

As her words sank in, Jackson's face tightened. "One of my ships. Jesus." He grabbed her hand and dragged her toward the door. "Come on, we have to find out which one."

Chapter Seven

Ysabel climbed in the truck beside Jackson and held on to the armrest as though her life depended on it. She didn't even squawk about leaving her car in the parking lot. Another reason Jackson admired his executive assistant. She knew. A car could be replaced, lives couldn't.

She buckled her seat belt and stared straight ahead, up for the challenge no matter what it was. "Where to?"

"Port of Houston." He had backed out and was racing down the street toward the interstate before he remembered to buckle his own seat belt.

"We don't know that's where he went," she stated.

"He's only got a badge to work with Champion Shipping vessels and equipment. If he's getting on a ship like his neighbor said, it has to be one of ours."

"Maybe he's just getting on a ship to catch a ride home, wherever that is." Ysabel had always played his devil's advocate, brainstorming with him on ideas that made his corporation grow and prosper.

She could be right in this case. The man might just be catching a ride home, but Jackson wouldn't bet on it. Gregor was a suspected terrorist. One of his compatriots had already died, obviously before completing his mission to blow up something besides himself. Jackson ground his teeth together but didn't reply. No use worrying Ysabel any more than she already was.

He didn't have to say anything, the woman was smart. "Same old Jackson Champion," she said, shooting him a tight smile. "You're not willing to risk the lives of your other employees if there's even a fraction of a chance he'll try something stupid."

"Right."

Ysabel pulled her BlackBerry from her purse. "Well, then, I'd better get busy. Because we don't have time to swing by the downtown Champion building to check our databases, I'll call the harbormaster at the Port of Houston and find out if any of Champion Shipping's freighters or petroleum ships have left the port today."

"I don't know what I'd do without you." He kept his words light, but his hands tightened on the wheel. With the threat of her resignation lingering between them, he'd have to learn how to do without her soon enough.

Ysabel didn't return his glance or respond to his comment about what he'd do without her, instead concentrating on her cell phone.

Her lack of response was more disturbing than if she'd responded to his statement. He'd thought they were almost back to normal after the scare at Gregor's apartment, trading sarcasm and insults, like two close friends. Had this latest scare set them back?

His hopes of keeping her on staff were dwindling drastically and he didn't know what to do to convince her to stay. Why did women have to be so damned difficult to understand?

Time to think about how to keep Ysabel later, the more immediate issue being Gregor. If the terrorist got on a petroleum ship, there was no telling what he'd do. Many of the petroleum ships left the port empty on the way to distant locations halfway around the world.

When he reached the freeway, he pressed his foot to the accelerator, giving the truck everything it had, pushing to the speed limits and over.

Ysabel ducked her head, pressing her ear to her phone with one hand and holding on with the other, asking for the harbormaster or anyone who could tell them which Champion ships had left the port that day. She dug in her bag for a pen and notebook, scribbling madly. When she was done writing, she spoke slowly and clearly, "Listen carefully. Contact the captains of those ships and find out if one Greg Voleski is on board." She paused, then continued. "It could be a matter of life and death. Call me as soon as you know." She gave him her cell number, clicked the BlackBerry off and sat staring straight ahead, her finger hovering over the Talk button on her phone.

The Port of Houston loomed ahead, the lights from the Barbour's Cut and Bayport terminals illuminating the sky like daytime. The port never slept, containers had to be moved day and night. New ships traversed the Houston Shipping Channel heavily loaded with cargo or fuel.

When Ysabel's phone buzzed, Jackson pulled to the side of the road, shifted into Park and rolled the window down to breathe in the smell of the water and listen to Ysabel's end of the conversation.

"Champion Shipping, Miss Sanchez speaking." She listened for a moment, pressing her phone to one ear and her hand over the other ear to block out all street noise. Then she looked across to Jackson, her face pale in the lights from the dash and the container yard. "Gregor's on the *Grand Aggie Four* petroleum tanker." Her focus shifted to the phone again and she repeated what she was hearing. "It's passing through the Houston Shipping Channel between Pelican Island and Port Bolivar right now."

Galveston. Jackson knew the area, it was a narrow strait through which ships entered and left Galveston Bay. A potential choke point for shipping traffic.

He reached for the BlackBerry, but before Ysabel could hand it to him, a distant boom filled the night air, cutting through traffic noise from the street beside them.

Ysabel yelped and dropped the phone. "What was that?"

His stomach lurched, cold dread washing over him. "Give me your phone." Jackson lunged across the seat desperately searching for the device she'd dropped.

She found it in the side pocket of the door and handed it to him, her hands shaking.

"Was that an explosion?" he yelled into the phone. All he could hear on the other end were people shouting.

"What's happening?" Ysabel leaned close, pressing her ear against his hand holding the BlackBerry.

"All hell's broken loose," he said, straining to understand the muffled shouts. Someone was shouting, "Call the Coast Guard!"

The harbormaster came on the line. "I have to clear this line for emergency response."

"This is Jackson Champion of Champion Shipping. What happened?"

"Your petroleum tanker, *Grand Aggie Four,* just exploded in the Houston Shipping Channel. Now please, I must clear the line so we can get to work." The line went dead.

Ysabel sat back in her seat, her face blanched. "He blew up the ship."

"That son of a bitch blew up my ship." Jackson tossed the phone in her lap and set the truck in drive, pulling a sharp U-turn in the middle of the road. He knew the captain of that ship personally, had discussed the nature of the shipping industry and the impact of terrorism at length over a bottle of the finest whiskey. They'd always known terrorism was a possibility, but when it hit one of your own…

Ysabel hung on to the door and her BlackBerry. "What now?"

"Call Tony Ingram."

"The helicopter pilot?"

"Yeah, we're going up to have a look."

She thumbed through her contact list stored in her phone until she found the pilot and punched in his number. "Mr. Champion requests your presence at corporate headquarters. Prepare the helicopter for flight, pronto."

Jackson kept one of his helicopters on the roof of Champion Shipping's headquarters building. He aimed his truck for that one now. The trip back to the heart of Houston took less time than the drive to the port terminals.

Ysabel thanked God the police force wasn't out in droves like they were during rush-hour traffic. When they arrived at Champion Shipping headquarters building, Jackson parked on the street in a no-parking zone and ran in, so focused on getting to the helicopter that he barely noticed Ysabel breathing hard, struggling to keep up with his longer stride.

He tossed the truck keys to the night security guard on the front desk. "Get someone to move my truck." And then he ran to the elevator.

The elevator dinged open immediately and he held the door, waiting for Ysabel to catch up.

When she tumbled through, gasping for air, he felt a twinge of guilt. "I'm sorry."

She held up a hand, sucked in a breath and said, "I know, you want to see what's happening." Another breath rattled into her lungs. "Me, too. I'm just out of shape."

With a quick glance at her slim figure with curves in all the places a woman ought to have them, he shook his head.

"Yeah, right, out of shape." He passed his access card through the elevator's lock mechanism and pressed the button for the roof. With nothing to do but wait for the elevator to climb to the twenty-first floor, Jackson had a chance to study Ysabel.

Her cheeks were pale and her shoulders drooped as though she were exhausted.

"You look all done in." He frowned. "Maybe you should go home."

"What?" She straightened, pushing her hair back behind her ears. Although some color returned to her cheeks, it didn't hide the dark smudges beneath her eyes. The woman was beat and Jackson felt responsible.

"You haven't been feeling well lately and what with the attack tonight—" He frowned. "I insist you catch a taxi home. Get some sleep. I can have one of the security guards escort you there."

"Madre de Dios!" Ysabel planted her hands on her hips, her green eyes sparkling in the muted elevator lights. "You may be my boss—temporarily, I remind you—but you're *not* my keeper. I know my body better than you do, so stop trying to tell me what I do and don't need."

Jackson's back stiffened. "You're as stubborn as a mule, did you know that?"

"Takes one to know one."

"Yeah, well, if I wasn't in a hurry, I'd make sure you went home." And tuck her in bed to make sure she actually went to bed. The thought of Ysabel in a bed made Jackson's heart pound a little faster.

"If I wasn't a lady, I'd tell you what you could do with your bossiness."

He snorted. "Nothing's stopped you before." Jackson's blood was pumping through his veins, his anger and desire rising with each word they batted at each other. Why did she have that effect on him? She made him mad enough to either shake her or kiss her. Both options held too much appeal to ignore.

Thankfully the elevator door opened before he could do either.

Ysabel was the first one out, pushing through the heavy metal exterior door to the roof, wind from the helicopter blades whipping hair into her face.

Jackson clamped a hand over his cowboy hat to keep it from blowing over the side of the building.

Sitting inside the helicopter, checking over the instruments, Tony Ingram waved them forward.

Jackson climbed into the front seat next to Tony. Ysabel slipped into the backseat and buckled her seat belt, praying her morning sickness didn't extend past eleven at night or morph into motion sickness. Maybe Jackson had the right idea and she should have gone home. The smell of aviation fuel was doing nothing for the stability of her stomach.

Then the thought of the people aboard the *Grand Aggie Four* being injured or killed brought her out of her own troubles and made her focus on the Houston skyline.

The helicopter lifted off and made a sweeping turn southeast toward Galveston, leaving Ysabel's stomach behind, or that was what it felt like. Lights from the Houston skyline twinkled in the blackness of the sky like a million Christmas lights lit up all at once. She barely noticed the city's beauty, instead concentrating on retaining the contents of her tummy, thankful she hadn't had more than a handful of crackers before leaving her apartment earlier that evening. So much had happened in between, she'd forgotten to eat.

Ysabel couldn't hear the words Jackson was saying to Tony, so she slipped the flight headset over her head, the reassuring crackle making her feel more connected in the noise of the aircraft.

"I don't see flames or anything yet," Tony was saying.

"Hopefully, you won't," Jackson replied, his voice mechanical and filled with static. "The ship was empty, on a scheduled run to Saudi Arabia."

Tony switched his mike to another frequency and then switched back. "Coast Guard's helo is up and they say they have boats in the water. Should be able to see something soon. I can't get too close with the Coast Guard down there working. I'll swing wide so you can get a view of all sides without interfering with other air traffic."

Jackson pulled out a pair of binoculars and peered out the window.

As Ysabel looked out at the lights stretching the length of Galveston, she zeroed in on the gap between Pelican Island and Port Bolivar. She'd been across that strait many times as a young girl on the ferry that connected the two strips of land.

The *Grand Aggie Four* sat still in the water surrounded by fire boats, pumping water onto the side and deck of the ship. Without binoculars, Ysabel couldn't estimate the amount of damage, but a dark smudge of soot stained the column of the bridge.

"Jackson, I have to cut this trip short," Tony said into the headset.

"Why? What's wrong?"

The tightness of Jackson's voice made Ysabel lean forward in her safety harness, craning her neck to see the instrument panels as if she knew anything about what they should look like.

"I'm losing oil pressure." Tony had a white-knuckled grip on the control stick.

Ysabel's heart thundered against her chest. "Is losing oil pressure a bad thing?" she asked, her voice crackling in her ears.

"Could be." Tony's gaze ran over the instruments and he leaned toward the window, peering out. "Damn. We must have blown a hose. You better brace yourself and look for a place to land."

Land? Ysabel looked out at the moonlight reflecting off the water of Galveston Bay. As far as she knew, helicopters didn't land on water.

Tony tilted the control stick toward the closest land. "I won't have much control, so get ready for a rough landing."

Ysabel clutched a hand over her belly. "Holy Mary, Mother of God," she whispered. How could this be happening?

The helicopter spun in circles, losing altitude at an alarming rate. Lights from Port Bolivar seemed to rush up at them in rotating swirls.

There were houses down there. What if they landed on one?

"Can you aim this thing for Fort Travis and the beach?" Jackson called out over the mike.

"I'm trying," Tony grunted, both hands on the stick, struggling to stabilize the spinning aircraft and direct it to a relatively clear landing area.

With her heart stuttering and her breathing coming in ragged gasps, Ysabel closed her eyes, praying to God to keep Jackson, Tony and her unborn child safe. The spinning motion continued, but she kept her eyes closed tightly.

"Brace yourself for impact!" Tony yelled.

Calm settled over Ysabel as she let her imagination carry her toward the earth. The bumpy swirling of the chopper was nothing more than the wind gently rocking her and the baby. When she opened her eyes, they would be on the ground.

One…two…three…

Ysabel opened her eyes as the helicopter hit with a bone-jarring thud. Metal crunched, the skids buckling beneath them. The body of the chopper leaned, setting the thundering blades at an angle. One hit the ground, snapped off and flew toward the sea, followed by another.

Ysabel tried to duck, but the restraints held her tight in her seat. With parts flying in all directions, all she could do was watch and hope none hit the people inside the helicopter.

The engine stopped, the broken blades rotated to a stop and stillness settled over the smooth grassy landscape of Ft. Travis historic park.

Then Ysabel took her first breath in what felt like hours. With the breath came panic. "Jackson?" When he didn't answer, she knew she had to get the heck out of the chopper. Her fingers clawed at the straps, searching for the buckle. At last she found it and released the catch. As soon as she was free of the restraints, she toppled forward, hitting the back of the seat in front of her. The door beside her jerked open and Jackson stood there, his eyes wild, his hat missing and his hair standing on end. He was the most beautiful sight to Ysabel.

He dragged her out of the chopper onto her feet and crushed her against his chest. "Oh, Jesus, I thought this was it." His hands roved over her body as if reassuring himself she was alive. Then he was kissing her, his mouth slanting over hers, his tongue delving in to taste hers. When he stopped long enough to breathe, his breath brushed against her cheek. "I thought I'd lost you." He kissed her again, this time taking it slow, as though he cherished every caress.

"You two all righ—" Tony rushed around the tail of the helicopter and skidded to a halt. "Uh…right?"

Jackson broke away from the kiss and stared down at Ysabel. "Are you?"

Her face flaming at being caught kissing the boss, Ysabel pushed against Jackson's chest. "I'm fine." When he didn't let go, she pushed harder. "Really, you can let me go." The more she pushed, the more panicked she felt as if his arms were chains around her. Her puny efforts were weak at best and to her horror, her eyes filled with tears. Dizziness made her head spin, mimicking the motion of the spiraling helicopter before it landed. If he didn't let go, she was afraid she'd throw up yet again. "Please," she begged, her voice choking on a sob.

His eyes narrowed and he eased his hold.

As soon as his arms loosened around her, she regretted her haste to be free. The spiraling sensation intensified and Ysabel's vision blurred. Without warning, her knees turned to noodles. *"Madre de Dios…"* she said as she crumpled to the ground.

Chapter Eight

"She's coming around," someone whispered.

"Delia?" Ysabel's eyes fluttered open to the soft lights of her own bedroom. "Delia? Is that you?"

"Shh, *mi hermana*. I'm here." Delia lifted Ysabel's hand and squeezed gently.

Images of the helicopter spinning to the ground blasted through Ysabel's memory and she sat up straight. "Jackson?"

"He's fine, the pilot's fine, you're fine. Lay back and sleep." Delia fluffed an extra pillow behind her and gently pushed her back against them. "You're not taking care of yourself. Mama will be angry that you are not taking very good care of her first grandchild. You won't hear the end of it when she gets back from Monterrey."

"Did I pass out?" Ysabel laid back, the soft pillows feeling wonderful after the crazy day. "What time is it? Or should I ask what day it is?"

"Relax. You've slept for only eight hours. You could use another ten, if you ask me."

Ysabel sat up again. "Eight hours!" She glanced at the clock on the nightstand. "I'm supposed to be at work." She shoved the sheet aside and swung her feet off the bed.

"You're not going anywhere." Delia stood in Ysabel's way

so she couldn't get out of the bed without running into her sister. "Doctor's orders. You're not to get out of bed until noon."

"Doctor?"

"Yeah, Jackson had his physician make a house call."

The blood drained from Ysabel's face and she lay back against the pillows. "Did he…"

"Tell Jackson you were having his baby?" Delia frowned. "No, but he should have."

"No." Ysabel pushed a hand through the tangled mass of hair. "I have to find the right time."

"You need to tell him soon. The poor man was beside himself, convinced you should be admitted to the hospital. But you kept telling him no."

"I did?" Ysabel smiled weakly at her sister. "I must not have been too out of it."

"You were out of it enough that Jackson stayed beside your bed until I arrived. If I hadn't pushed him out the door, he'd have stayed through the night. The man's a wreck."

Ysabel's heart jumped in her chest and then settled back into a slower rhythm. She knew better than to get her hopes up where Jackson Champion was concerned. Exhaustion was making her loopy. "He'd do that for any employee."

Delia shook her head. "I don't know. The man was worried enough to stick by you when he had a blown-up ship in the Houston Shipping Channel."

"He should have been out there."

"The doctor told him you'd be fine after a little rest, that you didn't need someone to babysit you. But did Jackson go out to check on his ship? No, ma'am. Not until I'd arrived and told him he had to leave or face the wrath of Delia."

Since when had Ysabel Sanchez become a liability to her boss? She didn't like it one little bit. She was an independent self-starter who didn't need anyone else. Yet at the back of her mind, she liked it a little too much. A girl could get used to having a man worry about her for a change. Any man but Jackson Champion.

"So?" Delia planted her hands on her hips. "What are you going to do about him?"

What was she going to do? She obviously had to tell him or he'd have her committed to a hospital and learn about the baby from someone besides her. She tapped a finger to her chin. Question was, when? "I'll tell him, but the timing has to be right."

Delia rolled her eyes. "As far as I'm concerned you've already passed the right time and gone straight to no-matter-when-you-tell-him-you're-screwed."

"How bad is it?" Akeem settled in one of the leather chairs in Jackson's office.

"No one died, except the man who set off the explosion, and the ship's not sinking." Two things he was relieved to learn early that morning when he'd finally gotten the first response personnel to fill him in. "It appears as if the damage is to the side of the ship. That's about all I know at this point. The Coast Guard won't let anyone on board until the accident has been thoroughly investigated. The crew has been evacuated and treated at local hospitals."

"In the meantime, you have to wonder if there are any more terrorists working at Champion Shipping." Flint McKade pushed his cowboy hat to the back of his head and rubbed his temples. "I don't like it."

Jackson turned to Akeem. "Have your people in Rasnovia found the two men identified as terrorists? I'm afraid what happened last night here in Houston could happen anywhere Champion Shipping assets are."

Akeem shook his head. "They've disappeared. However, my contacts in Rasnovia were able to get into their apartments. They left behind a computer that didn't work."

Jackson sat forward. "Where is it?"

"It's at the airport in Rasnovia, awaiting your orders. You'll have to smuggle it out. There's still so much unrest since Viktor's family was overthrown."

"I'll have a Rasnovia plane there within an hour to collect it." Jackson leaned forward and punched his intercom button to Ysabel, before he remembered she wasn't in.

"Yes, sir?" Ysabel's voice came over the line, clear and calm.

It took him a full five seconds to realize he shouldn't be hearing her voice, not until the next day. "What the hell are you doing back in the office?"

"Working," she said, her tone firm, her words terse and no-nonsense. "What can I do for you?"

Jackson's blood pressure rose and he would have told her off, but the curious faces of his friends made him reconsider. Instead he forced himself to rise slowly from his chair. "I'll be right back."

As he passed by his two friends, he could swear that out of the corner of his eye he saw Akeem shooting a grin at Flint. When Jackson turned and glared at the man, Akeem looked all innocence. The chuckles behind him did nothing to improve his mood as he pulled the door closed behind him.

Ysabel sat with her head bent in conversation on her cell phone.

Jackson waited, not very patiently, taking the opportunity to study her, while she concentrated on the caller's message.

Dark circles smudged the skin beneath her eyes and her arms looked almost painfully thin. Had she lost weight or had she always been that skinny?

An image of her naked in his bed flashed through Jackson's mind. No. She'd lost weight in the two months he'd been gone. Damn it! Why didn't she get off the phone and go home?

When she showed no sign of hanging up, Jackson grabbed her phone from her hands.

"What the—" She glared up at him. "Give it back."

"Miss Sanchez will call you back," he said into the phone and then he clicked the Off button.

She leaped from her seat and lunged for the phone, but it was too late. "Hey! That was Fielding from the FBI."

"I don't care if it was the man on the moon." He poked a finger at her. "You're supposed to be home in bed. Doctor's orders."

"I don't take orders from anyone."

"I'm the boss."

"We can fix that right now." She grabbed her purse from one drawer in her desk and a sealed envelope from another. "My resignation." She shoved the envelope at him.

Jackson refused to take it. "I have a contract."

Color flared in her cheeks like twin red flags. "Screw your contract." She slipped the strap of her handbag over her shoulder. "I can't take any more of your bossiness."

"You can and you will or I'll see you in court."

All the angry color drained from her face and Ysabel backed away a step, chewing her bottom lip, her eyes rounding like a deer in a face-off with a rabid hunter.

Where had the fighting tigress gone? From raging temper to scared to death in seconds, this woman was not the unflappable executive assistant he knew so well. "What the hell happened to you while I've been gone?"

Tears welled in her eyes and she appeared to be thinking about what she'd say. When a sob escaped her throat, she clapped a hand over her mouth. "You idiot." Then she turned and ran for the ladies restroom outside the door to the executive office suite.

"What the hell's going on?"

Tom Walker popped up from his desk on the other side of the spacious office. "Was that a rhetorical question or did you want me to follow her and find out?"

Jackson stared at the young man as though he'd lost his mind. "No, hell, no. I'll see to it." He followed Ysabel through the glass doors and into the hallway. The door to the ladies' room swung gently to a stop.

Determined to get to the bottom of Ysabel's problem, he stormed through the door.

One of his employees from accounting stood in front of the mirror applying lipstick. When she glanced in his direction, she gasped. "Mr. Jackson!" The lipstick she held clattered into the sink basin, leaving a long red streak of color against the porcelain. "What are you doing in here?"

"Oh, tell me he didn't come in here." Ysabel cried out from behind a stall door.

"Damn right I did." He glared at the woman retrieving her lipstick. "Get out."

"Yes, sir." She left the mess, lipstick and all, in the sink and scampered through the door.

With only one pair of legs showing beneath the stall door, Jackson rest assured he and Ysabel were alone. "Now will you tell me what the hell is wrong with you?"

"I don't know what you're talking about."

"Damn it, Ysabel! Get out here and explain yourself."

"I make it a point not to explain myself." A loud flush emphasized her words and she stepped through the door, her head held high, her eyes tear-bright. "Do you think it dignified for a man in your position to be standing in the ladies' bathroom?"

"Dignity be damned. I own the company and—" he caught himself before he said the first thing that came to his mind.

"And you own me? Is that what you were going to say?" Her gaze sharpened into slits. "I promise you, no one owns Ysabel Sanchez. Not you, not this company. No one." She stormed to the sink and twisted the knob hard, blasting a spray of water onto her hands.

"I didn't say that. I know no one owns you. I do, however, own a contract that binds you to this company for an additional two weeks."

"One week, five-and-a-half days."

"Whatever! While you work for me, I can tell you when you can be in or out of the office. I want you to go home now."

"If I leave this office, you have no control over my movements. I could go back to Gregor's apartment for all you know."

The sucker punch hit him square in the gut and he sucked in a breath at the thought of Ysabel back at that apartment where she'd been shot at. "You wouldn't be stupid enough to go back there, not after last night."

"You don't know anything about me, Jackson Champion."

"That place is now a crime scene. I know that you're smart and you wouldn't do anything to place yourself or any other Champion assets in danger."

"Oh, so not only do you own me, but you consider me a Champion asset? Well, you know what you can do with your assets." She stormed by him letting the door swing shut in his face.

Before he could push through to follow Ysabel, another woman from accounting entered the ladies' room, jerked to a stop and clapped a hand over her mouth. "I'm sorry. Am I in the wrong bathroom?"

"You could say that." Jackson ducked around her and shoved through the door. "Ysabel!"

He had to run to catch up to her at the elevator. She'd just punched the Down button and stood tapping her sexy foot against the granite tiles.

The elevator door opened, but Jackson stepped in front of Ysabel. "Where are you going?"

"You wanted me to take the day off, remember? I'm taking the day off."

The thought of her leaving the building without him

gripped his chest like a giant fist and squeezed. "No. I don't want you to take the day off."

"Make up your mind, Mr. Champion. I'm not a yo-yo on a string you can sling around."

"I don't trust you to go home to bed."

"That's your problem." She reached around him to keep the elevator door from closing. "Now, if you don't mind, I'm leaving."

"No, I need you to work."

She let go of the elevator door and crossed her arms beneath her breasts, the action pushing them upward, emphasizing their fullness.

Tired as he was, his body reacted to her stance by sending a jolt of energy to his groin. How could she have lost weight everywhere else and gained more cleavage at the same time? He didn't remember her breasts being so plump and heavy.

Jackson scrubbed a hand over his face, reminding himself she was an employee and he had no business staring at her in that way. He had no business making love to her two months ago or last night, for that matter. Hell, the lack of sleep, worrying over his ship, freaking out over crash-landing a helicopter with Ysabel in the back and then Ysabel passing out in his arms was making him crazy.

"Just come back to the office. You can ease back into work. In fact, I have something that needs immediate attention."

"Let Tom do it. He's quite capable."

"He doesn't know as much as you do. I need a plane to fly to Rasnovia within the next hour to make a pick up."

Ysabel's eyes brightened. The woman loved a challenge. "That won't be easy with all the unrest since the uprising."

"That's why I need you to handle it." He tipped his head to the side. "But if you think Tom can handle it, I'll let him. Of course, it could be a life-and-death mission for the pilot and that kind of responsibility is a lot to ask of someone with limited experience.

She nodded, her gaze shooting to a corner as if she was already thinking through what she'd have to do to make it happen. Then her eyes narrowed. "Don't think I'm going to change my mind about leaving Champion Shipping at the end of my two-week notice. I'm not."

"Understood." Jackson fought off a smile. The woman was stubborn but good and she couldn't resist a challenge.

When she turned toward her office, the bell on the elevator dinged, the door slid open and Jenna Nilsson stepped out.

Jackson smothered a groan. The last person on earth he wanted to see was his ex-fiancée. If it hadn't been for her dumping him two months ago, he'd never have slept with Ysabel, placing the huge strain on their relationship and threatening her future employment with Champion Shipping.

Ysabel turned toward the door, her eyes narrowing slightly. If Jackson hadn't been watching for her reaction, he might have missed it.

Jackson stared at Jenna, trying to remember what he saw in the woman. Granted she was beautiful and would make a beautiful decoration at dinners, but what else? She had been mediocre in bed compared to Ysabel's fiery passion. He'd never been in love with her. All he'd wanted out of the relationship was to check off a box on his list of things to do to prove his success. Marriage had been a taboo, certain to fail in his books, just like the majority of marriages today. He'd only taken the risk with Jenna because there was no love lost between them.

Since the day she'd walked out on him, he'd never been more grateful to anyone in his life. Dumping him had shown him what an arrogant bastard he'd become, thinking marriage was just another task to be accomplished.

His one night with Ysabel had shown him how wrong

he'd been. She'd told him how important marriage was, how he deserved love and his potential wife deserved it, as well. He hadn't been that upset about Jenna leaving because he'd never loved her, never could. He needed a woman who was his equal in intelligence, drive and determination. Someone who could stand up to him in an argument and give as good as she got. He didn't want a doormat to let him walk all over. Ysabel said he needed someone who would love him with passion and be his equal in all things.

It was that night that Jackson realized he needed to marry someone like Ysabel. Strong, confident, smart and beautiful. She'd always stood up to him when he was wrong, including when he announced he was going to marry Jenna. She'd been the one to point out that he was a fool to marry for anything other than love. If all he wanted was a pretty woman to grace his dinner table when he entertained, he could hire an escort service.

Ysabel had been with him for five years, refining his rough edges and guiding him through the social intricacies of doing business with people of foreign cultures.

With Jenna and Ysabel standing in front of him, Jackson knew beyond a doubt he could never marry a woman like Jenna and why he'd ever thought he could baffled him now.

When Jenna stepped out of the elevator, Ysabel fought the sudden urge to leap forward and shove her back in before the door closed behind her. Better yet, wait until the elevator dropped to the bottom floor and push her into the open shaft.

"Mr. Champion is very busy, Ms. Nilsson. Perhaps you could come back another time?"

Completely ignoring Ysabel, Jenna advanced on Jackson and slipped her arms around his neck, a determined glint in her eyes. "Hi, Jackie, aren't you going to say hello to your fiancée?"

Ysabel's back teeth ground together. Why this woman insisted on calling Jackson Jackie was beyond her.

"Ex-fiancée, Jenna." He unwrapped her arms from around his neck. "Remember? You dumped me for another man."

Her pretty pink lips pursed in a sexy pout, making Ysabel want to scratch her baby-blue eyes out. "You're not still mad about that, are you?" Her beautiful brows rose into her pale blond hair. "Jackie, honey, if you'd returned my calls, we could have straightened out this whole mess months ago."

"Maybe I didn't want to straighten out this mess as you call it."

Ysabel wanted to cheer at his words, but she kept her mouth shut. If she jumped on Jenna and scratched her eyes out, Jackson might get the hint that she had more than an employee's interest in the big boss of Champion Shipping. She didn't want that to come out, especially in front of the ex. No matter what, she couldn't appear jealous, catty or in love with Jackson in any way. Her break from his employment would be hard enough for her as it was. If he thought he could play on her emotions for him to try and talk her into staying, she'd be hard-pressed to fend him off. All he had to do was crook his finger and she'd probably fall right back into his bed. She was a sucker for the Champion charm. As evidenced by her present condition.

"Can we go somewhere to talk?" Jenna shot a pointed glare at Ysabel. "Alone?"

"I'm sorry, Jenna. We have nothing to talk about. Ysabel—Miss Sanchez is right. I'm too busy right now."

The blonde's pouty lips slimmed into a narrow line. She sucked in a deep breath and forced another smile. "Why don't I stop by later this evening at your condo? We really need to talk."

"Seriously, Jenna." Jackson hooked her arm and steered her toward the elevator. "I don't have time and I meant it. It's over."

Her voice rose, her eyes widening. "You can't mean that."

"I assure you, I do."

Ysabel fought to keep a smirk from lifting the corner of her mouth. The woman deserved to be tossed out on her butt. After dumping a man as beautiful as Jackson Champion, she should be committed for evaluation in a mental institution.

Rumor had it she was involved with another man while she'd been dating Jackson and that she hadn't given up the other man even after Jackson asked her to marry him. She didn't deserve Jackson Champion.

And you do?

Ysabel's shoulders sagged.

He stood in front of her talking softly to Jenna as he firmly placed her in the elevator.

Jenna's face pinched into a frown. "Jackie, honey, really, we should work things out. We make a beautiful couple. Think of how beautiful our children will be. Please, Jackie, at least have dinner with me."

Ysabel's breath caught in her throat at the image of Jenna and Jackson having little blond-haired children with blue eyes. He couldn't go back to Jenna. He had a child on the way with her, Ysabel. Didn't he realize what a mistake having children with Jenna would be?

To Jackson's credit and Ysabel's relief, the man shook his head. "It'll never work." Then he punched the Down button. As the doors closed he turned to face her.

Ysabel's face flooded with heat. She'd been staring at him and his ex the entire time. And thinking he couldn't have children with anyone else was just wrong, when she planned on leaving him and taking his child with her. She spun and would have dashed back to her office, but Jackson stuck out a hand and snagged her elbow.

"Whoa, wait a minute."

"I'm on my way to place that call. Is there anything else you want?"

He held her elbow and stared down into her face. In a low, deep voice, he answered, "I want so much more."

Mesmerized by his tone, Ysabel had to remind herself to breathe. If he insisted on being this close to her for the remaining time of her two-week notice, she'd be back in his bed before nightfall and she could do nothing to stop herself. "I'll work for you until my two weeks are up, but don't touch me ever again." She jerked her elbow free and fled before she threw herself into his arms and begged him to be her one and only.

He didn't reach for her, didn't try to stop her as she ran from him. Part of her wanted him to, the other part knew what a mistake it would be.

Fool! She was a complete fool! For the past five years, she'd fought her growing attraction for the man she called boss. All that pretense had been a complete waste of time. She was a goner and the sooner she got the hell out of his office and life the better. She was just an executive assistant. He was a billionaire! *Get a grip and get on with your life, girl.*

Ysabel sat behind her desk and pretended not to notice Jackson as he passed her and entered his office.

She'd make her call and leave, unable to trust herself in his presence, not with her hormones intensifying every emotion. Pregnancy was making her crazy.

After she'd arranged for an airplane from a nation other than the good old U.S. of A., and in particular, Champion Shipping, she hung up the phone, grabbed her purse and headed for the door. Her cell phone rang before she made it out of her office.

"Ysabel, it's Mitch."

Ysabel dropped back into her seat. "What have you found?"

"Not much, unfortunately. Detective Green is keeping a tight rein on all the information about your man Voleski even to the point he isn't sharing it with the FBI agent."

"That's odd."

"No kidding. I can't dig too much without alerting Green to my activities. You might have to do some digging on your own. You have information about him through your company. Start there."

"Thanks, Mitch. I will." She clicked the Off button and sat tapping her pen against a notepad.

"Anything I can help you with?"

Ysabel spun her seat to face Tom and an idea came to her. "Tom, check Greg Voleski's employment data and find out what bank he does business with. He should have a routing number listed on his direct deposit. Chase it down and see if it leads anywhere else. You know, transfers to other accounts, deposits to his account other than from Champion Shipping payroll." Ysabel's lips twisted. "Can you do that?"

Tom grinned. "I shouldn't tell you this, but I once hacked my way into an account in the Cayman Islands. It was easy." He held up his hands, his eyes rounding. "Don't worry. I know right from wrong. I didn't steal anything. I just happen to love a challenge."

Her lips curled into a smile as she gathered her purse. "Consider this a challenge. Anything you can find on Greg Voleski or Gregor Volsky will help."

Ysabel left the office. She had no intention of going home to bed when she had some checking to do of her own. If the detective wasn't sharing information, she had to get it for herself. She'd be damned if she let Champion Shipping take the fall for the terrorist attacks. Not that she had any obligation to help Champion Shipping when she planned to quit in one week and five days. But still, Jackson didn't deserve the fingers pointing at him and the Aggie Four Foundation.

When she stepped out of the elevator into the parking garage below the building, she passed a sheriff's deputy SUV sitting in the handicap parking zone. Detective Green sat in the driver's seat talking to someone in the passenger seat. Ysabel couldn't see the face of the person on the other side, but she could see long blond hair. Detective Green shot a glance her way, his eyes narrowing.

Ysabel shivered. To say his look was cold would be an understatement. Glacial fit the description. She hurried to her car and slid behind the wheel, pulling out of her designated parking place. Once outside the parking garage, she drove up the street, made a U-turn and waited on the opposite street corner to see who came out. If the detective exited, she might catch a glimpse of the person he was talking with. Why she cared, she didn't know, but somehow it seemed important. So she waited.

The wait didn't last long. A silver BMW slid out of the parking garage and onto the street.

From her vantage point, Ysabel could clearly identify the driver—Jenna Nilsson, combing a hand through her long blond hair. Hadn't she left the building more than twenty minutes before Ysabel? Was she the blonde Detective Green had been talking to in the front seat of his SUV? If so, why? What did she have to do with the case?

Ysabel made a mental note to ask Jackson when she saw him the next day. In the meantime, she headed for Greg Voleski's apartment in the shadier part of Houston. With it being daylight, she should have no troubles. It was times like last night that got sticky.

Before she made it to the street where Gregor had lived, her BlackBerry chirped and Tom's number displayed on the screen. Nervous tension washed over her and she passed the street she should have turned on. Tom's call could mean good news. Maybe he had something for her that would save her from going to the apartment where she'd been shot at the night before?

Then again, Tom's news could be more of the same—bad news for Champion Shipping.

Chapter Nine

Jackson sat in his chair behind his desk glaring at the desk calendar. When had Ysabel become so aggravating? If she'd just do as he told her, everything would be fine.

"Anything we can help you with, buddy?" Flint asked, a gleam twinkling in his eye.

Jackson glanced up almost surprised at the presence of his two friends. He'd been so deep in thought, he'd completely forgotten that he'd called a meeting of the Aggie Four. "We need to get this whole situation under control before the Aggie Four Foundation is blamed for everything." If he could solve his corporation's issues, he could spend time figuring out how to get his life back in order. And Ysabel. Huh! Like he could manage that woman.

"We agree. While you were out *counseling* your employee, Flint and I turned on the news."

Jackson glanced toward the screen mounted on the wall opposite his desk. The screen was black. "What, are they ripping Champion Shipping to shreds over this latest fiasco?"

Flint nodded. "Pretty much."

"And if that wasn't enough, they're putting two and two together and coming up with five. They've included the Aggie Four Foundation in the accusations, not to mention tying everything back to political unrest in Rasnovia. The

Rasnovian rebels are claiming responsibility for the explosion on the *Grand Aggie Four.* The news reporters aren't going to let you off so easily."

If the paparazzi thought they could milk a story, they would milk this one for all it was worth. "Great." Jackson pushed away from his desk and stood, running a hand through his hair. "What next?"

A light tap on the door and Tom poked his head inside. "Mr. Champion, a Detective Green is here to see you."

Akeem's lips twisted into a grimace. "You had to ask."

Jackson didn't want to have anything to do with Detective Green. The man had been nothing but antagonistic toward him since the explosion on the dock. He'd rather work with Special Agent Fielding of the FBI than Detective Green. He sighed. "Show him in."

Tom backed out of the way.

Detective Green barged in like he had every right to be there. "Jackson Champion, I need you to come down to the station for questioning."

"I've already given my statement to Agent Fielding of the FBI."

"Are you refusing to come with me?" Detective Green thumbed the handcuffs tucked into his thick utility belt.

"I'm not refusing anything. Unless you have a warrant for my arrest, I'll come down to the station in my own vehicle, on my own time. You're not parading me through the offices like a criminal again. I put up with it once. Next time I'll have your badge."

Red stained Detective Green's neck, climbing up into his cheeks. "You think you can walk all over regular people like they mean absolutely nothin'? It always has to be your way, doesn't it? You just intimidate or buy your way out of anything. You rich guys think you can get away with making promises you don't intend to keep, regardless of the consequences. Well, I call bull. Someday really soon, you'll get what's coming to you."

Jackson raised his hands, surrender style. "I have no idea what you're talking about. Have I done something to offend you in any way?"

"I'm tired of you wealthy SOBs getting away with murder."

"Whoa, slow down there, cowboy. Are you accusing me of murder now?" Jackson stepped toward the man, his fists clenched. "Because if you are, I'll sue you for slander faster than you can say 'Your honor, I royally screwed up.'"

"I'm not accusing you of nothing. But if you don't get down to the station in the next hour, I'll have that signed warrant to arrest your ass." Detective Green glared at the others in the room and then stalked out, slamming the door behind him.

"What the heck just happened here?" Akeem asked, his jaw hanging open.

"Looks to me like Detective Green's got a bug biting his butt about something." Jackson relaxed his fists.

Flint stared at the closed door, his brows high on his forehead. "No kidding."

Jackson planted his hands on his hips. "I get the feeling it's more than just investigation of this case."

"You're not going down to the station are you?" Flint asked. "He's liable to throw you in jail for just looking at him."

"I'll get my attorney to pave the way. I'll see if Agent Fielding is around, as well."

"Sounds good. Want us to come with you?"

"No, that's not necessary."

"Then I'll be at the ranch, ready at a moment's notice," Flint slapped Jackson's shoulder and grinned. "Stay out of jail, will ya?"

Akeem stuck out his hand to shake Jackson's. "I'll be at the auction house. Let me know what you find out about that computer. And if you need me for anything…"

"I know, all I have to do is send up a flare and you two will be here." Jackson smiled. He could count on his friends.

Flint and Akeem left, promising to think back through all that had occurred in the past few months leading up to the explosion on the *Grand Aggie Four.*

Jackson followed Akeem and Flint. Outside his office, he rounded the corner to Ysabel's desk, intending to take her home before he stopped in at the sheriff's office. Her chair was empty. "Damn!"

His hand on the door exiting the executive suite, Akeem stopped in his tracks and turned. "What's wrong?"

"Ysabel's gone." Jackson slipped his cell phone from the case clipped to his belt and punched the speed dial for Ysabel. After several rings, the call rolled over to her voice mail. "Damn." He glanced around the office. "Tom!"

Tom's head bobbed up over the top of his five-foot-tall cubicle walls. "Yes, sir."

"When did Ysabel leave?"

The younger man disappeared and reappeared outside of his cubicle. "About an hour ago."

"Did she say where she was going?"

"No, sir. But I might have an idea." He paused long enough to make Jackson grind his teeth.

"Well?"

"Before she left, she told me to dig into Greg Voleski's employment file for the bank he had his check direct deposited to." Tom shot a look at Flint and Akeem.

Jackson nodded. "You can say anything in front of them. I trust them implicitly."

"She told me to find out anything I could about bank deposits, transfers or anything under Greg Voleski's accounts." Tom shuffled his feet. "I don't know if I should be telling you this."

Jackson stopped himself from reaching out and shaking

the younger man. "Ysabel told me you're an excellent hacker and this is an emergency. What did you find?"

"He transferred all his money from the account where his check was deposited into another account under the name of Anna Chernov. And that's not all. A sum of two hundred fifty thousand was also deposited to Ms. Chernov's account the day before yesterday."

"Where did the two hundred fifty thousand come from?"

"I'm working on it. Face value, the money looks to be from a charitable foundation from some foreign country. But the more I dig, the shadier it gets. Corporations owned by other corporations, owners that can't be traced and hidden or numbered bank accounts in the Caymans and Switzerland. It's a veritable jigsaw puzzle."

Tom handed Jackson a sticky note. "That's the address of the woman here in Houston whose account Greg Voleski dropped his money into."

Jackson closed his eyes and inhaled deeply. "Bottom line is that you gave Ysabel this same address, am I right?" He opened his eyes and pinned Tom with a stare.

Tom sighed. "Yes, sir. She might have gone there."

"Thanks." Jackson spun on his heels and raced for the elevator, Akeem and Flint jogging to keep up.

Once in the elevator, Jackson's toe tapped against the tiled floor, a million scenarios spinning through his head, none of the outcomes good for Ysabel.

"Need help on this one, Jackson?"

"Maybe. Did you two ride together?"

"Yes," Akeem answered.

"If you could swing by Ysabel's apartment to see if she made it home, that would be great. Call me when you get there and let me know." As he handed them the address, the elevator doors slid open into the parking garage. Jackson climbed into his pickup; Akeem and Flint spun out in Flint's

Diamondback Ranch truck. Out on the street, they turned in opposite directions.

Jackson punched the address into his GPS and followed the directions, navigating through the streets to southwest Houston, the neighborhood with one of the highest crime rates in the city. The sun crept toward the horizon too fast for Jackson's comfort. He hoped he got to Ysabel before she did something stupid, like get out of her car.

YSABEL stared out at the cracker-box house with faded, peeling pink paint. Somewhat safe inside her air-conditioned car she'd retrieved earlier that day from Gregor's apartment building, she was glad she'd gotten it back relatively unscathed from its night in a less-than-safe part of town.

The late-afternoon sun slanted over a huge oak tree in the front yard, casting long shadows over the rotted eaves and patched roof. Bushes crowded around the sides and front, growing as tall as some of the windows, shrouding them in mystery. In the front yard, a rusted-out car tilted into the dirt on three dry-rotted flat tires and one missing wheel. The hood stood open, the engine as rusted as the paint job.

The place reeked of the desperately poor. Having grown up on the edge of just such a place, Ysabel's heart leaned toward pity for the woman she'd come here to see. Anna Chernov. The woman Gregor Volsky had left his last dime to—granted, two hundred and fifty thousand dollars couldn't be considered pocket change.

A group of young men, probably teens, dressed in droopy pants and oversize T-shirts with a picture of a snake twisted across the front, loitered at the corner bus stop across the street. If she wasn't mistaken, they were watching Ysabel watching the pink house. Should she get out or should she call the police and let them handle this?

Her gut told her the police should handle this.

A curtain flickered in the front window and a woman's face peered through the dirty glass, an infant clutched to her chest. The fear in her eyes couldn't be mistaken. The curtain jerked closed and the house grew still.

Would she try to run out the backdoor? If this woman disappeared, they might never know anything about who deposited the large sum of money into Gregor's account the day before the ship exploded. Blood money for blowing up the *Grand Aggie Four*. The woman hiding behind the curtain might know something that could lead the police in the right direction—away from Champion Shipping and the Aggie Four Foundation.

Before she could change her mind, Ysabel flung open her door and ran for the house. At the front door, she pushed the doorbell and listened. Nothing. The bell didn't work, not that it surprised her. As far as she could tell, the house didn't even have central air. An old window unit tilted out of a small window on the side of the house, its quiet stillness evidence it didn't work. As hot as it was, the woman and her baby had to be steaming all closed up in the house.

Ysabel knocked on the door. "Anna, please open the door."

A baby cried out in the back of the house and a door slammed.

Her heart kicked up a notch, sending her blood pounding through her veins. Ysabel raised her hand to knock again, changed her mind and ran through the overgrown grass to the back of the house.

Ysabel stepped up on the broken concrete of the back stoop and glanced through the glass window on the backdoor.

A small woman with dark hair and pale skin juggled a baby in one arm and a large suitcase in the other, pushing it through the kitchen toward her. When she saw Ysabel, she screamed and dropped the suitcase. The baby wailed in her arms as she ran for the front of the house.

"No, don't run!" Ysabel cried out. She jiggled the doorknob and the door swung open. "Anna, wait!" Ysabel raced after the woman, afraid Anna would hurt herself or the baby she carried in her hurry to get away from the stranger at her backdoor. "Please, Anna, I won't hurt you."

As the frightened woman reached the front of the house, the living room window shattered, a bottle topped with a flaming rag crashed into the wall above a sagging plaid sofa.

The smell of gasoline filled the air and the entire living room burst into flames.

Anna stood transfixed, staring into the fire, tears streaming down over the bundle of baby in her arms. She wailed in a language Ysabel didn't understand but guessed to be Russian.

With the fire rapidly spreading around her, Ysabel had to do something fast. She grabbed the woman around the waist and hauled her through the small house to the backdoor.

Afraid whoever had attacked the front would now be at the backdoor, Ysabel shoved Anna and her baby to the side and she flung the door open, ducking back into the kitchen. Smoke billowed into the kitchen gagging her. It was die in the flames or face whatever was waiting for them outside.

Ysabel chose to take her chances. She clutched Anna's arm and dragged her through the door and out into a back alley. The wind chose that moment to swoosh down among the trees and they were enveloped in a veil of smoke, giving them a chance to get away from the house without being seen. Once they reached the corner of the house two doors down, Ysabel pulled Anna into a crouch, hiding behind a large rollaway trash bin.

The wind shifted and died down, the smoke swirling upward. Fire engulfed the small-framed house, eating away at the chipped paint and bone-dry wood. The flames leaped into the darkening sky, catching in the towering oak, lighting it like a giant torch.

Anna curled up beside Ysabel, coughing, her eyes filled with tears. The baby cried softly until Ysabel took it in her arms and spoke soothing words to it until it quieted.

Too afraid to move and disclose their location, Ysabel waited in silence until fire-engine sirens wailed in the distance.

Whoever had thrown the Molotov cocktail into the house would leave or at least not attempt to cause them more harm with the police and firefighters arriving on the scene.

Ysabel pulled out her cell phone and called a taxi. She'd get Anna someplace safe and then figure out what to do next.

As she waited for the taxi to arrive one street over from the fire she turned to the woman who'd almost died in that house.

"Anna, what do you know about Gregor?" Ysabel held the baby, rocking it back and forth to keep it from crying.

A sob escaped the woman and she buried her face in her hands. "He's dead. Gregor is dead."

Ysabel laid a hand on Anna's arm. "I'm sorry. You must have cared for him a great deal."

Anna looked across at the baby in Ysabel's arms. "My baby's father is dead."

Although Ysabel should have guessed it, Anna's words struck her hard. The baby in her arms would grow up without a father.

Anna clutched at Ysabel's hand. "Gregor wasn't bad man. He was afraid. So afraid…" The woman doubled over, sobs wracking her body.

"What was he so afraid of?"

"A man…" Anna struggled for a word, "How you say make him afraid for life?"

"Someone threatened Gregor?" Ysabel's arms tightened around the baby.

"Yes! He tell Gregor he kill him and his family if he not do what man want."

"What did he want Gregor to do?"

Anna looked around the ground as if trying to form the right words. Then she made sounds of an explosion, her hands rising into the air. "Make big boom. Fire, lots of fire."

"Is that why he blew up the ship?"

Anna shook her head, more tears falling from her eyes. "No, he refused to make explosion. He blew up the ship and himself to make police see."

"To get their attention?" Ysabel asked.

Anna nodded, tears glistening in her eyes. "And to keep bad man from hurting me and Katiya." She bent over, her tears choking off her words.

Ysabel's head spun, her stomach tightening into a knot as she absorbed what Anna was telling her. "He blew up a ship to keep from having to blow up something bigger?" Ysabel's voice was barely above a whisper, cold trickling across her heated skin.

"Yes."

Chapter Ten

Four blocks from the address he'd entered into his GPS, Jackson came to a halt in traffic. Tapping his thumb on the steering wheel, he wondered what the heck had caused cars to come to a complete stop in a residential neighborhood.

The longer he sat, the more panic seized him. He checked his GPS for the remainder of the directions, pulled his truck to the side of the road and jumped out. People sitting in cars with their windows rolled down, shouted and honked at the traffic stopped dead in the road.

Jackson jogged past the line of vehicles, his pace quickening with every step. He turned left at the next street and looked ahead at a towering column of smoke rising from the tops of the houses. "Ysabel!" When he reached the street where Anna Chernov lived, several fire engines filled the narrow lane. Smoke billowed from the burned-out remains of a house, now nothing more than a blackened skeleton of a frame. Hoses trained a steady stream of water into the smoldering ashes. In front of the house stood a soot-covered compact car that may once have been red, a string of rosary beads hanging from the rearview mirror.

"Ysabel." Jackson pushed through the gawkers staring at the house until he reached a police officer. "Sir, were there any people inside?"

"Keep back, sir, and let the firemen do their job."

"I have to know, was there anyone inside that house?" Jackson grabbed the man by the collar to get his attention. "For God's sake! Someone I care about might have been in that house."

The cop's lips formed into a straight line. "Let go of the collar, mister."

Jackson dropped the man and stepped back, running a hand over his face, staring into the glowing embers being soaked with water. "I have to know."

The cop straightened his collar and sighed. "I'll see what I can find out. Wait here."

Jackson stood right where the cop told him and waited for the longest two minutes of his life, while the cop spoke with the fireman in charge.

The fireman spoke words Jackson couldn't hear and shook his head.

Jackson's chest tightened until he couldn't breathe.

The cop picked his way back through the crowd of rescue workers, stepping over the swollen water hoses. When he found Jackson, he shook his head. "As far as the firemen can tell there was no one in or around the house when it burned. We won't be certain until they can sift through the debris and that won't be until it cools. Probably tomorrow morning."

Jackson chose to cling to the hope that the preliminary investigation was correct and that no one died in the fire. If that was the case, where was Ysabel and why was her car still here?

With the scent of ashes clogging his senses, Jackson circled the neighborhood, searching for Ysabel. After thirty minutes, he gave up and headed back to his truck. The stranded cars had found alternate routes and dispersed, leaving the street clear for Jackson to turn around.

Pressing his foot to the accelerator, he sped back into the heart of Houston. He had to find Ysabel.

CLOSE to midnight, Ysabel climbed out of the taxi in front of her apartment building, smelling of smoke and exhausted beyond reason. If someone wanted to kill her at this point, she might welcome it gladly.

Her hand rose to her belly, a faint tightening in her uterus reminding her she really had to think more about her baby. From here on out, she would stick close to home and not go chasing after suspects or witnesses or anyone else even remotely dangerous.

She'd spent the last hour and a half settling Anna into a women's shelter her cousin Rita volunteered at. No one spoke Russian there and, for some misguided reason, Anna clung to Ysabel, refusing to let her go, as if she were a lifeline in a raging sea. Ysabel promised to stay with her until she fell asleep.

Anna had lain on a full-size bed, with baby Katiya next to her. Katiya cooed and waved a chubby fist, but the clean diaper and a belly full of warm milk worked its magic and eventually the baby had drifted to sleep, with her mother not far behind. Ysabel stared down at the two, wondering if she'd end up like Anna, in a women's shelter because she didn't have a job and couldn't find a job to support her baby.

Leaving Champion Shipping depressed Ysabel more than she'd let on to her sister, because leaving Champion Shipping meant leaving the only man she'd ever loved.

Tired but too jumpy from being attacked yet again, Ysabel sat in the backseat of the taxi, wondering what she was going to do for a car, a home, and a life after she quit her job in one week and four days. Options swirled in her mind, but none stuck. She'd worry about it tomorrow. Tonight she needed sleep.

With a weary smile at the security guard on the front desk, she dragged herself into the elevator and punched the button for her floor.

The upward motion almost made her long to sink to the

floor. The only thing holding her up was the handrail and the thought of picking herself up from the ground when the elevator stopped. She'd be better off collapsing in her own bed than on the elevator floor. What would the neighbors think?

The bell dinged at her floor and the doors slid open. Dog-tired, Ysabel stepped off the elevator and gasped.

Leaning against her door was a tall Texan, arms crossed over his chest, his cowboy hat pulled down over his forehead, making his eyes unreadable. Jackson Champion.

Ysabel stopped dead still. Blood raced through her veins, jump-starting her tired body. God, he looked like heaven. If only he were there because he loved her. If only he wasn't just coming to check on his *assets*.

She squared her shoulders and marched right up to him. "Excuse me, you're blocking my door." She reached out with her key, intent on unlocking the door and diving in before he opened his mouth to tell her what he thought of her little disappearing act.

Her hand didn't make it to the door. He caught it in his and held it.

She tried to pull her hand free, but he held firm. "Let go of me."

"Tell me that wasn't your car in front of what's left of Anna Chernov's house." He yanked her to his chest, his arm wrapping around her waist like an iron band, his eyes achingly intense. "Tell me you weren't there and I'll let you go."

As Jackson's gaze burned into her, Ysabel's knees melted and she almost fell. The strain of the day and those darned hormones kicked in, pushing tears to the corners of her eyes. Why couldn't she control her emotions any better than she was? Falling apart in front of *him* was *not* an option. She wouldn't.

Darn it! She was going to fall apart. "Jackson Champion,

why don't you just go away and leave me alone?" Her voice broke on a sob and she leaned her head against his chest.

"I can't." The arm around her middle tightened. The other slipped up her back, his hand tangling in her hair, tugging her head backward until she was forced to look at him. He leaned forward and kissed the tip of her nose. "You have a black smudge on your nose. Soot, right?" His grip in her hair tightened. "Why, Ysabel? Why can't you stay away from trouble?"

She laughed, the sound ending on a sob. "It seems to be following me." Her hand slid up his shirt, bunching in the material. A girl could get used to leaning on all that muscle, letting him take on the world for her. As tired as she was, Ysabel was more than tempted. With a sigh, she laid her cheek against him. His heart thumped against her ear, mirroring her own, the steady beats fusing into a matched rhythm.

"What happened at Anna Chernov's?" he asked, tucking a strand of hair behind her ear.

"I'm so tired, can I tell you later?" If she didn't lie down soon, surely she'd fall.

"Give me your key."

Without a fight, she handed over the key, refusing to give up the support of his arm and body. He turned her, fitting the key in the lock. When the door swung open, he scooped her up into his arms and carried her across the threshold.

"Better be careful, someone might think we were newly-weds," she muttered in a low voice. Ha! Like that would ever happen. More tears sprang to her eyes. Jackson Champion marry his executive assistant? Those kinds of happily-ever-afters only happened to spineless princesses in fairy tales, not to independent tough girls from the barrio.

Jackson's arms tightened around her. "So what? Would that be so bad?"

A lump choked Ysabel's throat and she swallowed hard, daring to look up into his eyes so close to her own. "You heard that?"

A smile spread across his face. "You're right here, what did you expect?"

"For you to be gentleman enough to ignore my hysterical ramblings." She struggled against his arms. "Put me down. I can walk on my own." Even though she forced her voice to be firm, she wasn't all that certain she could walk on her own at this point. Being carried never felt so good and pride aside, she'd be better off letting him.

Jackson kicked the door shut behind him and headed directly for her bedroom.

The closer he got, the harder her heart pounded in her chest. Exhaustion flew out the window, replaced by hot, pounding blood, pumping adrenaline throughout her body. Another scenario wrapped around her senses, the one where he'd carried her to his bed in his condo two months ago. The scenario that ended in his making love to her throughout the night. That particular story had ended in Jackson's disappearing act and her own discovery that she was pregnant with his child. Hers was no fairy tale with its requisite happy ending. Hers was the one that led to heartache and loneliness.

When he passed the bed and entered her bathroom, Ysabel put her foot down. "I can take it from here."

"Are you sure? Your track record over the past couple days hasn't been stellar, you know." He let her feet drop to the floor, but he retained his hold around her middle.

Leaning on Jackson Champion was wonderful, his strength seeping into her, taking over when her own knees refused to support her. But she couldn't rely on him to always be there for her. She had to depend on herself.

"Really. I can manage on my own." *And I will manage on my own with a baby when you are long gone.* "Now get out of here so I can get a shower."

"Okay, but I don't like leaving you. What if you pass out again?"

"I'm not going to pass out." *Unless you continue standing in front of me.*

If he stayed this close, she might hyperventilate. Or worse, she might hold her breath to keep from telling him she loved him and was carrying his child. That would be a huge mistake. The last thing she wanted was Jackson Champion feeling obligated to marry her or suing for custody of their unborn child. "You know where the door is, just lock it on your way out." She shoved him through the bathroom door and closed it between them. Then she leaned against the door, pressing her heated cheek to the cool wood paneling.

"I don't hear the water going," Jackson said, as if he were standing right in front of the door. "Can't shower without water."

"I don't need you telling me how to take a shower." An image of him running a wet soapy cloth over her breasts shot through her mind. He'd bathed her in his shower a lifetime ago, touching and caressing every part of her. Ysabel stifled a moan. Why did she have to dredge up all those old memories now? Something tightened in her lower belly and it wasn't her uterus. She wanted Jackson to throw open the door and do again what he'd done before. It took every ounce of internal strength to keep from opening the door and dragging him inside. "Go away, Jackson," she called through the door, her tone half-hearted at best.

"I'm going."

For several long seconds, she didn't hear a thing. For the first time since she'd had it installed, Ysabel was hating the wall-to-wall carpeting throughout her apartment that muffled every step Jackson took. When a door opened and clicked shut, she let out the breath she'd been holding. The man who'd completely complicated her life was gone. Or was he?

Ysabel peeked out the door of the bathroom. Her view of the apartment was limited to what she could see through her bedroom door. She didn't hear anything or see anything move. Good. A nudge of disappointment ached in her empty belly. After a quick shower, she'd fix something to eat. She had to stay healthy for her baby.

Leaving the door to the bathroom ajar, she stripped and climbed into the shower, closing the sliding glass door. Jackson's presence, along with his intriguing blend of aftershave lingered in the bathroom.

As she soaped herself, her imagination replaced her own hands with his, sliding down over her naked breasts. A moan rose from her throat. How she wished she hadn't been so hasty in throwing him out. With raging hormones completely unbalanced by the baby growing inside her uterus, she felt hotter, sexier and more turned on than she'd ever felt in her life. And what did that get her? Alone and naked in a shower, wishing for something she couldn't have. Tears spilled down her cheeks, mingling with the spray from the shower. Sobs wracked her chest and she leaned against the shower wall, unable to cope with the world weighing down on her shoulders.

Wrapped so completely in her misery, she didn't hear the shower door slide open. Not until Jackson stepped into the shower behind her did she realize he was there.

Strong arms pulled her against his blue chambray shirt. A big calloused hand pushed the hair out of her face and kissed the tears from her eyes.

"I thought you left." She laid her face against his damp shirt and inhaled the scent of Jackson.

His hand circled her waist and drew her naked hips against the rough denim of his jeans. "I'm glad I didn't."

She should be angry he hadn't gone, but she wasn't. Too tired to care about tomorrow, Ysabel sighed. "Me, too."

His mouth descended to claim hers, his lips sliding across, wet and warm. When he pushed past her teeth, he dived in, plundering her hungrily.

Warm water sprayed Ysabel's back, a heat more intense built inside. Clumsy fingers fumbled at the buttons on his shirt, eager to feel his skin against hers.

He pushed aside her hands and jerked the buttons loose.

Ysabel peeled the shirt over his shoulders, the heavily soaked fabric dropping with a plop to the tub floor. The jeans were next. She flicked the metal button loose and slid the zipper down, her gaze scraping along the opening. She almost came undone when she realized he'd gone commando, wearing no underwear at all.

His erection jutted forward through the opening, strong, straight and pulsing with his need. Jackson stripped the jeans off and gathered Ysabel in his arms, pulling her against the full, naked length of him.

Her soft skin reveled in the warm hardness of his muscles, the coarseness of the hairs on his chest and legs.

Jackson reached for the shampoo and squirted some into his hands, gently massaging suds into her long, smoky hair.

Ysabel closed her eyes and leaned back into the spray, the bubbles sliding down over her breasts. Heavier than bubbles, Jackson's lips followed their path, taking one turgid peak into his mouth, sucking gently.

Something deep inside tugged at her with each pull of his mouth on her nipple. Tension spread throughout her body.

With a hand full of soapy lather, he smoothed her body with large, sensual circles, trailing ever downward to that juncture of her thighs, aching for his touch.

She opened her legs to him and his hand glided between, cupping her sex. His finger stroked her folds, sliding across the ultra-sensitized nub of her desire.

When he fingered her there, Ysabel gasped, her hands climbing his shoulders to wrap around his neck. She pressed her hips closer, wanting more of his exquisite torture.

He flicked his finger over and over until she was practically climbing up his body to be closer still.

Ysabel intertwined her fingers around his neck and pulled his head down to kiss her, her hands sliding across broad shoulders. Her movements were spasmodic, erratic like the spasms of her nerve endings down there. Every part of her burned with her need to have Jackson inside her, filling her, loving her until she forgot all about tomorrow. Forgot about leaving him and starting over somewhere far away. Right at that moment, she wanted him and wouldn't stop until she had him.

His hands cupped the back of her knees and he lifted her, pressing her back against the cool tiles of the shower walls.

She wrapped her legs around his waist, anticipating the pressure of him inside her.

Poised at her entrance, he paused, dragging in a shaky breath. "I have protection in the back pocket of my jeans."

"No need," Ysabel gasped. "I can't get pregnant. Please, Jackson." She eased down over him, his full length sliding into her, the delicious friction making her breath catch in her throat. "Ah."

He paused. "Am I hurting you?"

"Yes, by stopping you're killing me." Pushing down on his shoulders and flexing her legs, she rose up and then eased back down. "Please, Jackson, make love to me." Normally, she hated begging, but now wasn't the time to be normal. Now was the time to throw caution and all her inhibitions to the wind and just *feel*.

Jackson braced her against the wall and holding her hips

in his big, capable hands, pumped into her, his movements strong and decisive. His lips pressed into a line of deep concentration, his head thrown back, his eyes half-closed.

His unrelenting strokes pushed her toward the edge and over, her body bursting with sensation.

Jackson drove into her one last time, buried deep inside her and held her there for a long, breathless moment. They stayed that way until Ysabel's legs slid down his sides. The brief spurt of lusty energy waned and she leaned into Jackson's neck.

He lifted her into his arms and pushing aside the sliding glass shower door, set her on the floor. With a large fluffy towel, he dried her from head to toe, squeezing the moisture from her long hair.

Too tired to think, Ysabel let him. His gentle caresses lulled her into a state of sleepiness she could no longer fight. When his hand smoothed over her belly, she could imagine him pressing his ear there to listen for the beat of their baby's heart. Jackson would make a good father. He deserved to know about his child. And she needed to tell him about what Anna had told her about Gregor.

When she opened her mouth to spill her guts, he surprised her by swinging her up into his arms and carrying her into her bedroom. He laid her among the sheets, pulling the comforter up around her. She couldn't remember when it had felt so good to be in bed. The warmth and comfort caressed her naked skin, reminding her of how tired she was.

Then he slid in behind her, spooning her body against his, her butt pressing against him, his hardness still apparent. If only she had the energy.

Her eyes drooped. She was going to tell him something. A yawn pushed the thought out of her head. What was it?

His arm curled around her, a hand cupping her breast. His breath stirred the drying hair behind her ear.

Tomorrow she'd remember what she wanted to tell him. Tomorrow was soon enough. Ysabel snuggled deeper into his arms and drifted off to sleep, the sound of a baby's cry drawing her into her dreams of a maid marrying a prince, where happily-ever-afters really did happen to girls like her.

Chapter Eleven

Jackson lay awake for a long time after Ysabel drifted off to sleep. The longer he lay there, the more his chest hurt. The events of the past two days crowded his thoughts, the uppermost being the near-misses on Ysabel's life. He had to do something to keep her safe until this mess was sorted out. The Aggie Four was under attack. Ysabel was a target, as well. Someone wanted her dead.

His arms tightened around her and she burrowed closer. He inhaled the scent of her herbal shampoo and the soap he'd used to clean her body. The woman was an enigma. For the first five years he'd known her, she'd been the model executive assistant, following the rules of boss—employee relations to the letter, with a little attitude to make it interesting. More than interesting. When Jackson had slipped up and gone to her, following Jenna's rejection, he hadn't expected to act on his desires where his competent assistant was concerned. He'd been as surprised as she was when he'd taken her into his arms and kissed her. Her passion enveloped him in a fire he couldn't douse and…well…that had been the end of his platonic relationship with Ysabel. Now that he knew what heat lay beneath her cool, no-nonsense facade, he couldn't forget.

His hand skimmed over her breast, the nipple tightening

into a hard bead. He didn't want to forget. He wanted more from her than polite conversation over a desk. What he wanted was to make love to her on the desk. Hard, fast, explosive passion. His blood quickened, racing through his veins.

Ysabel stirred against him, reminding him that she needed sleep, not to be woken to slake his selfish desires.

He closed his eyes, willing his lust to abate. An impossibility with her soft skin pressed against his thickening member.

Surely if he concentrated on what was more important than making love to Ysabel, he'd cool the heat.

Why would someone want Ysabel dead? She wasn't the billionaire. She wasn't involved in orchestrating the rebirth of Rasnovia with the Aggie Four Foundation. That had been the members of the Aggie Four. If a terrorist was out to bring down his band of friends for helping a struggling nation, why involve Ysabel?

After two hours, Jackson slipped from the bed and gathered his saturated clothing. He stuck them in Ysabel's washer on spin cycle and then tossed them into the dryer. While he waited for his clothes to dry, he paced her living-room floor, working the problem in his mind.

Two terrorists on U.S. soil. Both dead after trying to destroy Champion Shipping property. Two more in Rasnovia, loading bomb-making materials aboard Champion Shipping cargo ships. Had any more bomb materials slipped by the authorities? Did the terrorists have sufficient supplies to wreak havoc on U.S. soil? An icy shiver shot up his spine, making the hairs on the back of his neck rise to attention.

Another problem that guaranteed he wouldn't sleep was the knowledge that the gunfire at Gregor's apartment wasn't Gregor shooting at them to keep them from discovering anything among his personal belongings. At the time of the shooting, Gregor had to have been aboard the Grand Aggie

Four to orchestrate the explosion. Which meant another terrorist in Houston. Who could it be? None of his other employees had surfaced in their search. If he wasn't on Champion Shipping payroll, he'd be harder to find than the others. With over two million people in the city, the police and FBI would have a hell of a time tracking down one person.

Jackson performed an about-face and strode the length of Ysabel's living room floor. He'd get with Special Agent Fielding tomorrow and run through everything he knew and see if the FBI had any more information than he did on the mysterious shooter. Was the shooter the same one who'd tried to run them off the road the night before? Was he also the one who'd burned Anna Chernov's house to the ground tonight? Was it one man or a group of men?

With more questions than answers swirling through his mind, Jackson came to the conclusion that he needed help. Help finding the shooter. Help finding out who had paid Gregor to sabotage Champion Shipping. But most of all, he needed help protecting Ysabel.

Trouble was that he didn't trust anyone but himself to watch over her. He'd have to make sure she stayed with him every hour of every day until they caught those responsible for the attacks.

Jackson paused in the doorway to Ysabel's bedroom.

She lay curled on her side, naked to the waist, her hand resting across her stomach. Her straight brown hair splayed across her pillow, dark lashes emphasizing the shadows beneath her eyes. Full breasts, tipped with rosy-brown nipples pressed together, tempting him beyond redemption.

If he took on the responsibility of protecting Ysabel, how could he maintain the distance required of a boss to his employee? He hadn't managed in the past two days, so could he even hope to now that he knew her body, her passion?

Even as he pondered the dilemma, his groin tightened. A smile pulled at the corners of his mouth. Even Ysabel struggled to keep her distance, in a tug-of-war between pushing him away and holding him close.

A strange sense of satisfaction washed over him. She had feelings for him. As quickly as the satisfaction flowed through him, it ebbed away. Ysabel's conscience must be playing havoc with her work ethic. That had to be the reason she'd given her notice. Her honesty and integrity had been the reasons he'd hired her in the first place.

How could he keep her at Champion Shipping, knowing an affair with the boss went against everything she believed in? How could he let her go when he wanted to hold on to her forever?

Like now. The urge to hold her in his arms overwhelmed him, pushing him forward when he knew he shouldn't. Jackson climbed into the bed behind her, pulling her against him.

She turned toward him and pressed her face into the curve of his neck, nuzzling at the pulse beating there like a snare drum in a marching band. When her breasts pressed against his chest, he groaned.

He shouldn't have crawled back in bed with her, because now that he was there, he couldn't make himself leave.

YSABEL woke to the smell of food cooking in her kitchen. Her stomach rumbled in protest at being totally empty, the acids churning dangerously.

She stretched across the bed, rolling onto the opposite pillow that still smelled of Jackson.

Ysabel sat up straight, noticing for the first time that she had no clothes on. Heat burned in her cheeks and she grabbed for the sheet.

Jackson appeared at the door, a tray in his hands. "As

soon as you've had breakfast and get dressed, do you think you can manage a day at the office?"

Ysabel clutched at the sheet, her mouth going dry at the sight of him in nothing but jeans, his chest and feet bare. "Yes," she squeaked, cleared her throat and tried again. "Yes, of course." She cringed at her proper tone. What they'd done last night was anything but proper.

"Good." He strode across the room and set the tray in her lap.

She had to drop one hand to balance the tray. The sheet slipped low over one nipple.

Jackson leaned over her and tucked the sheet under her arm. Then he surprised her with a kiss on the tip of her nose. "Hurry up then. I made scrambled eggs and toast. Hope that's the way you like it."

Normally Ysabel ate eggs any way they came. Lately, even the sight of an egg made her stomach flip. She fought to control her gag reflex. At least until Jackson left the room, which he didn't seem to be in a hurry to do. She held the tray with one hand, her sheet with the other and stared up at him, her brows raised.

For a moment Jackson stood there. "You don't like scrambled eggs? I'm sorry. I should know that by now."

"It's not that."

"Is the toast overdone?"

Ysabel smiled, secretly thrilled that he wanted to please her.

"No, the toast is perfect." She pulled the sheet closer. "I've never eaten breakfast in bed."

"Never?"

"Not that I can remember. Certainly not naked." There, she'd said it, and the heat bloomed in her cheeks.

"You've been through a lot, you deserve to pamper yourself. But I get it. You want me to vamoose." He turned for the door. As he left the room, he glanced over his shoulder and gave her a wicked smile. "By the way, your sheet slipped on the left side."

Ysabel glanced down to where one of her breasts was fully exposed. "Why, you!" She dropped the sheet, grabbed a pillow and flung it at him.

He ducked out, his chuckle echoing into the living room.

Ysabel set the tray aside and climbed from the bed, glancing nervously toward the open doorway. She grabbed panties, a shirt and trousers from her closet and ran for the bathroom. Why she should be self-conscious about being naked in front of Jackson, she didn't know. He'd seen every part of her body now, more than once.

Her skin tingled in memory. A girl could hatch a few expectations out of his repeated attentions and Ysabel couldn't let that happen. Once she had her clothes on and downed a bite of dry toast, she'd have it out with Jackson and tell him that under no uncertain terms could they do again what they'd done last night.

Dressed, combed and having downed half a cup of decaf coffee and a slice of toast, she headed for the living room and the confrontation she fully intended to have.

Jackson stood at the window overlooking downtown Houston, with his back to her, his cell phone pressed to his ear. "That's right. I want a full security system installed by tonight. Can you do it? If not, I'll call around and see who can." He paused. "No, I trust that your people will give me a good deal. You've always come through for me before. Yeah, what are friends for? Thanks, Deke." Jackson hit the Off button, turned and ran his gaze the length of her. "Good, you're ready."

"Who was that?" Ysabel asked.

"A friend."

"What security system?"

"It's not important."

Too concerned about their fray into forbidden territory the previous night, Ysabel let the subject drop and thought about what she'd say to put an end to their indiscretions.

Before she could summon the courage to tell him she didn't want him to make love to her again, he hurried toward the door. "Grab your purse and let's get out of here."

"But we need to talk."

"Can we talk on the way to the office?" Jackson opened the door and held it for her. "Special Agent Fielding is meeting me there in twenty minutes."

"I'll take a taxi to pick up my car—"

Before she could finish her sentence, Jackson gave a grim shake of his head. "I believe your car was totaled last night. The fire at Anna's spread to your car."

With the door wide open, Ysabel stood transfixed. She didn't have a car. Last night she'd been too exhausted to gauge the ramifications and worry then. In the light of day, reality struck her. Without a car, she didn't have the independence she cherished so much. She needed to call the insurance company and get that ball rolling. If the damage was as bad as Jackson indicated, the adjuster would total her car, the one thing she'd hoped would last a lot longer. It had been the perfect car for her. It was paid off.

Quitting her job and not knowing how long it would take to find one even comparable made her stomach knot. She'd have to secure a loan within the next week and four days. The chances of getting a loan after she quit her job would shrivel up and blow away entirely. Not to mention, she hadn't banked on making a payment. That would cut into her finances considerably.

Jackson settled her in the passenger seat of his pickup and rounded the front of the truck to climb in. After he cleared the maze of the parking garage and emerged onto the street, he leaned back and glanced her way. "What was it you wanted to talk about?"

Ysabel sucked in a breath and let it out. Where to start? "About last night…"

"I'm sorry. I shouldn't have taken advantage of you while

you were so emotionally distraught. It wasn't fair of me and certainly not fair to you. Do you forgive me?"

Ysabel wished he wasn't being so nice. How much easier would it be if they were arguing and flinging accusations back and forth? Then she could blurt out the whole truth and not feel like such an incredible fool.

"It wasn't your fault. I'm equally to blame." She turned toward the window, avoiding his gaze. Now how would she say the rest?

"There, then that's settled."

"No, not really. You know it can't happen again, don't you? Promise me we won't do that again…." She twisted her fingers together in her lap.

"If that's what you want, I'll respect your decision."

"Good." She shot a glance at his profile, the toast in her stomach churning, ready tears springing to her eyes. She'd be damned if she let them fall.

Was leaving her alone that easy for him? Keeping her hands off Jackson was near to impossible for her. Thus the need to put distance between them, quickly. "I'll need to find a new car today."

His lips firmed into a straight line. "That'll have to wait. I need you at the office. Work is piling up and I can't afford for you to be out right now."

"But I can't function without transportation."

"Don't worry. I'll get you where you need to go after work." His tone brooked no argument. Traffic around them thickened, requiring all of Jackson's attention.

Ysabel sat back in her seat. Jackson playing chauffeur was not a solution to her problem. How could she maintain her distance if he insisted on driving her back and forth to work? As soon as she got to the office, she'd do some car shopping online. And when she'd put in her required eight hours at the office, she'd take a taxi to the dealership. Problem solved.

A trickle of relief spread through her, tempered by the knowledge that she still had to get through a day working for Jackson.

ONCE in the Champion Shipping corporate offices, Ysabel headed for the ladies' room, giving Jackson the perfect opportunity to set his plan in motion.

As he walked by the manager trainee's desk, he barked, "Tom, in my office."

The younger man shot out of his desk as though his butt had been loaded with a spring. "Yes, sir."

Once inside, Jackson closed the door and crossed to his desk before speaking. "I have a special project for you."

Tom's tense shoulders relaxed. "Great! What is it?"

"You're to stick to Miss Sanchez like fly paper."

"Yes, sir. Is there something in particular you want me to learn from her?"

"No. I just want you to keep her from leaving the building without my knowledge."

A frown pulled Tom's eyebrows together. "May I ask why?"

Jackson inhaled deeply and let it out. "Last night someone tried to kill her."

"Holy crap!" Tom's eyes widened.

"I don't think she quite realizes how much danger she's in, and it's up to the two of us to keep her from putting herself in harm's way."

Tom popped to attention and came very close to saluting Jackson. "Yes, sir! I'll stick to her like you said…like fly paper. Uh, sir?"

"Drop the sir, Tom. Call me Jackson. What is it?"

"What exactly is fly paper?"

"Never mind, just don't let her out of your sight."

"Got it." Tom performed a perfect about-face and left the office, his gaze panning the area for his new assignment.

Jackson smiled. He liked the kid. Maybe he'd make a good replacement for Ysabel, if she followed through with her threat to quit Champion Shipping.

Not that anyone, least of all Tom, could replace Ysabel.

Jackson sat behind his desk and stared at the mounds of paperwork that had accumulated in his inbox over the past two months. Ysabel kept him informed and in the loop on any major decisions via phone and fax. Today, he didn't have the focus to tackle any of it. Life-and-death threats tended to push finding the cause of those threats to the top of his priority list.

A light tap on the open door brought him out of his musings. Ysabel stood in the doorway, her cheeks unnaturally pink. "Mr. Champion, Special Agent Fielding is on his way up to see you."

"Good, when he gets here, show him in. And you'll need to stay, as well."

Her brows rose. "You need me?"

"You'll need to fill him in on what happened last night. You know, the fire, Anna Chernov?" His voice softened. "In case you don't remember, you were too tired to tell me everything. Actually, you were too tired to tell me anything."

Ysabel blushed and ducked out to meet the agent at the elevator.

A smile teased the corners of his lips. She'd been shy this morning about his seeing her naked. Now she was blushing over his comment about last night. He liked that.

His smile faded when Special Agent Fielding walked through the door. Jackson stood and rounded the desk to shake the man's hand. "Anything new on your end?"

Fielding's eyes narrowed. "Yes, but I'm not sure if it means anything."

"Then just spit it out."

"As you might have noticed, I'm getting little to no help from the sheriff's department. More particularly, Detective Brody Green."

"I'm not surprised. He's been nothing but antagonistic toward me from day one."

"Exactly. And it's been like pulling teeth to get information from him concerning the case." The agent inhaled and let it out. "I ran a check on him."

"And?"

"He's run up a debt to the tune of three hundred thousand dollars."

Jackson whistled. "That's a lot of cash on a detective's salary. You think he's feeling the strain?"

"That's my bet."

"You think he might be a little resentful of your fortune?" Ysabel entered the room, closing the door behind her.

"Could be."

She tapped a finger to her chin and stared out the window. "The question that begs to be answered is what does it have to do with this case?"

Fielding shrugged. "Maybe nothing." He turned his focus to Ysabel. "Jackson told me over the phone that you had a little excitement last night."

Ysabel nodded. "A little."

Agent Fielding pulled a pad and pen out of his pocket. "Start from the top and tell me everything you saw, heard and even smelled. I'd ask why you haven't spoken to the sheriff on this yet, but given Detective Green's demeanor, I can't say I blame you."

Ysabel nodded and glanced at Jackson before she began. She told him about receiving a tip that Gregor had a friend named Anna Chernov. She didn't enlighten him as to where she'd gotten the tip, just that she went to Anna Chernov's house on the southwest side of Houston. She filled him in on what Anna had told her about how she'd been afraid, what she'd said about Gregor sacrificing himself to save her and the baby.

"Where is Ms. Chernov now?"

Ysabel looked from Jackson to Fielding and back. "I'm sorry. She made me promise not to tell a soul where she is. She's afraid whoever started the fire at her house last night will find her and finish the job."

Agent Fielding nodded. "Is there a way you could set me up with a meeting with her, away from where she's staying?"

Ysabel nodded. "I'm sure I can."

"Good. Let's make that happen, let's say," Fielding glanced down at his watch, "four hours from now?"

Ysabel looked to Jackson. "I'll need transportation."

"You'll get it," he replied.

"Then four hours it is." She exchanged cell-phone numbers with the agent and arranged to call with the meeting location later.

"Back to the fire." Agent Fielding leaned closer. "Did you see anyone hanging around the house before you entered or after you left?"

Ysabel closed her eyes.

Jackson noticed the dark circles had barely abated after her night's sleep. He vowed to make sure she got to bed earlier tonight and to leave her alone so that she could actually sleep. Assuming she let him inside her apartment, otherwise he'd be sleeping in the hallway. He wouldn't leave her alone again.

"When I was still in my car outside Anna's house, I noticed a group of young men, maybe teens hanging around the corner across the street."

"Can you describe them?"

"They were wearing those baggy jeans with the crotch hanging down to their knees."

"Anything else? What about shirts, hair, piercings? Anything."

"All of them wore big T-shirts with a snake on the front."

Fielding sat back in his seat and jotted a note on his pad. "The *Culebras*."

Jackson's chest squeezed tight. "Aren't they one of the most violent gangs in Houston?" He shot a glance at Ysabel.

Ysabel's hand rose to her stomach, her face pale. "I've heard about them."

Jackson felt sick to his stomach, too. Ysabel had been within spitting distance of one of the most notorious gangs in the city, known for drive-by shootings, stabbings and gang rapes. His gut tightened at what had almost happened to her and what could have if the gang had gone into that house before they set it afire. His grip tightened on the pen he held until his knuckles turned white.

Fielding nodded at Jackson without voicing the many dangers of being in gang territory, his eyes saying it all. "I'll get my people on it immediately. Someone is bound to have seen them, maybe even know some of them we can bring in for questioning. In the meantime, Miss Sanchez," his gaze shifted to Ysabel, "I wouldn't go anywhere near the area, especially alone."

She held up a hand. "Don't worry. I've sworn off all investigation on my part. Last night convinced me to leave it to the pros."

Jackson wished he could believe her. But knowing Ysabel as well as he did, he knew her independent nature might get her into trouble yet again. Between himself and Tom, they should be able to keep up with her. He hoped. What more could he do? Physically tie her down?

Akeem's words came back to him. What about a bodyguard? He pulled a pad of paper close and jotted down a note to call Deke. The man had contacts in the security business. Maybe he could recommend a reliable source. He'd steered him in the right direction to having a security system installed in Ysabel's apartment. She'd be mad he went behind her back to have it installed, but maybe not so mad when he told her it was at the company's expense, not hers.

"Is that all you have at the moment?" Fielding stood and tucked his pad and pen into his jacket pocket.

"No, that's not all." Jackson nodded to Ysabel. "Could you call Tom inside?"

She left the room, closing the door behind her.

"I'm worried about Miss Sanchez," Jackson said as soon as the door closed. "Three attempts on her life in the past two days is three attempts too many. Can you look into that angle, as well?"

"Sure will. Did you make a list of those people who might have it in for you? Or events that could have made someone mad?"

Jackson sifted through his drawer and surfaced a sheet of paper he'd been making notes on. "I've been in business for over fifteen years and nothing besides the uprising in Rasnovia came to mind."

"I read in the paper that you and your fiancée split two months ago. Do you think she might begrudge your relationship with Miss Sanchez?"

Jackson stared at Agent Fielding as if he'd grown horns. "What relationship? Until Miss Nilsson called off our wedding, I didn't have a relationship with Miss Sanchez, not that any of this is your business."

"If it means finding the person responsible for the attempts on Miss Sanchez's life, it's my business. In most cases, victims are killed by people they know. Was Miss Sanchez familiar with Miss Nilsson?"

"She knew her and met with her on occasion. It was bound to happen because Miss Sanchez is my executive assistant." Jackson shook his head. "But I can't see Jenna Nilsson as a murderer."

Fielding shrugged. "I'll check into it. I'm sure you're

right, but it won't hurt to do a little digging into her background."

Ysabel knocked and opened the door, leading Tom into the room.

"Yes, Mr. Champion?" The young man walked in, darting nervous glances at Special Agent Fielding.

"Relax, Tom. I want you to tell Special Agent Fielding what you've learned so far."

Tom gulped. "You want me to tell him?"

"Not how, but what." Jackson turned to the FBI agent. "Tom has it on good authority that Gregor Volsky received a sizable deposit into his account recently. Isn't that right?"

Tom let out the breath he'd been holding. "That's right. Over two hundred thousand dollars two days ago."

Fielding looked from Tom to Jackson. "I take it I'm not supposed to ask how you know this."

Tom looked to Jackson.

"Right. But if I were in the FBI, I'd have all of Greg Voleski and Gregor Volsky's accounts frozen and start tracing those deposits."

Agent Fielding pinned Tom with his stare. "You mean your *authority* hasn't informed you of the source of the deposit yet?"

"No, not really." Tom stood straight, clasping his hands together in the front, clearly uncomfortable with the questioning. "Only that it was from a numbered bank account in the Cayman Islands. I can get you that number if you'd like."

"Yes, I'd like." Agent Fielding pulled his pen and pad from his pocket and jotted down some notes. "Tell your source thanks and if he ever wants a job with the FBI to give me a call."

A grin stretched across Tom's face. "Yes, sir!"

Jackson frowned. He didn't want to lose Tom now that he'd proven to be so useful. Then again, he'd never hold the guy back from the glamorous job of being an agent for the FBI. "Tom can get you that number for the bank account on your way out. Let me know what you find out about the fire last night."

Agent Fielding nodded. "I will."

Jackson stood. "And if it's all the same to you, Agent Fielding, we'd rather you didn't let Detective Green know where you learned about the money transfers."

The FBI agent touched a finger to his temple. "You got it."

Tom and Ysabel turned to follow the agent.

"Miss Sanchez, a moment, please," Jackson said, feeling strange calling her Miss Sanchez when he'd seen her naked just that morning.

Ysabel grabbed Tom's arm. "Don't you need Tom, as well?"

"Not now. I need to speak to you alone."

Tom glanced down at her hand on his arm. "Are you okay, Miss Sanchez?"

Ysabel's hand jerked free of Tom's arm as if she just realized she'd been holding him back. "Yes, yes. I'm all right. Go ahead. I'll be fine, just a little shaky from the fire last night."

"Want me to get you a bottle of water or something from the cafeteria?" Tom asked.

Jackson's back teeth ground together. "I'll take care of it, Tom. You can go."

Tom gave Ysabel one last look and left.

Ysabel stayed where she was for a long moment facing the door, her back to Jackson. Then she turned, her shoulders stiff. "What did you need, Mr. Champion?"

"I need you to cut the bull. After last night, we should be on a first-name basis, *Ysabel.*" When she refused to correct what she'd called him, he shrugged. "Fine. That's not why I called you in here."

"What is it then?"

"I want you to take me to Anna Chernov."

She stared right at him, no expression on her face. "I can't."

"You can and you will."

"I'm sorry, Mr. Champion, I made a promise to her that I would tell no one where she is."

"You don't have transportation."

"I plan on remedying that as soon as I get off work."

"You need to take me to her now. I'm afraid whoever attacked her last night might find her before we get her to a safe location."

"She's safe where she is."

"Are you willing to bet her life on it? And the life of her baby?"

Ysabel chewed her lip, a frown knitting her brow.

"I thought not. Now take me to her so that I can get her to a safe location."

Chapter Twelve

"I don't make a habit of breaking my promises," Ysabel groused in the seat beside Jackson. "Turn left at the next corner."

"You're doing her a favor." Jackson negotiated the turn. "Besides, you don't have a car, you might as well let me get you there."

"Which reminds me." Ysabel's fingers tightened around her purse strap. "After we get Anna situated, could you drop me off at the nearest car dealership? I need to purchase a new car."

"You don't just walk into a car dealership without a clue as to what you want in a car and how much it's worth."

"That's easy for you to say. You've got a vehicle. Try being without one, even for a day." She tapped her fingernails on the armrest. "It'll make you crazy."

"If that's what's bothering you, I'll help you find a car tomorrow."

"No, I want to find my own car by myself."

Jackson didn't respond, but his grip tightened on the wheel, his knuckles turning white. Had her response hurt him or made him angry?

Not that she should care. The main reason she wanted to find her new car by herself was because she didn't want a car that reminded her of Jackson. Especially after she'd left

Champion Shipping and Jackson behind. The split would be hard enough without constant reminders. With a baby coming, she'd want to talk about the safest car with the easiest access to a child's car seat. All these things she needed to consider, now that she was expecting a baby. It was just as well her car burned up. A compact car wasn't necessarily the best choice for a new mom with a baby and a bulky car seat.

As they neared the road where the battered women's shelter was located, Ysabel wished she'd been more firm with Jackson. Anna might not trust her again. "Stop here."

Jackson glanced around at the small homes that didn't look big enough for a shelter. "Is this it?"

"No, it's two blocks from here, but I want to go in alone and talk with her first." She held up her cell phone. "I'll call you when I get to Anna's okay." Ysabel reached for the door handle.

His hand shot out and he grabbed her arm. "No. I won't let you go there by yourself."

"And I won't destroy that woman's trust in me. If she knows that I led someone here after promising her I wouldn't, she might run. How do you want this to go?"

"I don't want you to go by yourself."

"I'd prefer you stayed here until I return." She could tell by the stubborn set of his jaw he wouldn't consider that an option at all. Ysabel sighed, making a decision she hoped she wouldn't regret. "If you can't manage that, then follow me on foot, and *don't* let anyone see you. And when I get Anna to come out, head back to the truck so that she doesn't know you followed me to her."

"I don't like it." Jackson's grip on her arm tightened, almost to the point of being painful, but Ysabel kept her silence, letting him stew over his choices. "Okay, I'll follow at a distance."

Ysabel slipped out of the truck and leaned back in. "Give me a chance to get ahead of you before you follow."

Jackson nodded.

She turned to walk away, her thoughts on what she'd say to Anna to convince her it was all right to talk with the man her husband had tried to destroy.

Before she'd gone two steps, Jackson called out. "Ysabel."

Her steps faltered and she turned back toward the truck.

Jackson leaned against the hood of the vehicle, his feet crossed at the ankles looking sexy and relaxed. But the tightness of his jaw indicated the effort it took for him to stay put. "Be careful, will ya?"

She held up her hand with her cell phone. "I'll call if I get into trouble." When she turned away, she couldn't help the smile that lifted the corners of her lips. In his own way, Jackson Champion probably cared for her. Warmth spread inside her chest, hurrying her forward.

Not that relationships lasted with Jackson. He'd proven that time and again. Hadn't she seen the parade of women over the past five years, moving through his life like they were moving through a revolving door? None of them stayed. He didn't let them.

Except for Jenna. When he'd decided it was time to settle down, he'd made his decision to marry Jenna and she'd been the one to back out. He hadn't been emotionally scarred by her rejection, more matter-of-fact than anything. Not that Jenna was his type at all.

And who was his type? The little voice in the back of Ysabel's head taunted her. Another little voice answered, *Me! Me! Me!*

Keep your feet on the ground, girl. Jackson Champion is a player, and don't you forget that.

Fully aware of the man trailing her to the point the hairs on the back of her neck stood at attention, Ysabel tried to concentrate on what she'd say to Anna.

When she arrived at the shelter, she entered through the front door. Mrs. Rodriguez, the home's administrator called out from her office. "If you're looking for Anna, she left an hour ago."

Ysabel's stomach dropped. "Did she say where she was going?"

"She said something about a bank and money. Her accent was so thick, I barely understood her."

Nausea threatened Ysabel's finicky pregnant stomach. "Did she say when she'd be back?"

Mrs. Rodriguez checked her watch. "About now. She was only going to be gone for an hour. She left Katiya with me and I'm sure she'll wake up hungry before long." Mrs. Rodriguez waved to the playpen on the far side of her desk where a sleeping baby lay curled up in a blanket a fist pressed against her cheek. The baby jerked, as if sensing their attention, and then settled, her mouth making little sucking motions.

Ysabel's heart melted at the sight of the baby. Soon she'd have one of her own. Would she look like Jackson? In some ways, Ysabel hoped not. Forgetting Jackson would be hard enough without the constant reminder. But deep in her heart, she really hoped her baby would have his dark hair and blue eyes.

"There she is now." Mrs. Rodriguez's gaze focused on the window.

The front door opened and Anna stepped inside, her face and hair covered in a light scarf. When she saw Ysabel standing there, she rushed forward, wrapping her thin arms around Ysabel. "Oh, Miss Ysabel, I am happy to see you."

Ysabel hugged the woman and set her aside. "Can we go to your room and talk?"

Anna glanced at Mrs. Rodriguez.

"Go." The older woman waved her away. "Katiya is still sleeping. I'll bring her if she wakes."

Anna led the way to the back of the house where her small room was located.

Once inside, Ysabel closed the door and turned to Anna. "Are you all right? Are they treating you well?"

Anna smiled, nodding her head. "Yes, oh, yes. Mrs. Rodriguez has been very good to me and Katiya." Her smile faded and her brows pulled inward. "But I cannot repay her."

"She said you just went to the bank. Were you unable to access the money Gregor left you?"

"The bank tell me the account is frozen. I have no money and I can't get any more." She clasped her hands in her lap, tears springing to her eyes. "How can I pay for food for me and Katiya?"

Ysabel didn't like the idea that she'd been to a bank and liked it even less that the account had been frozen. If Tom was able to hack into Gregor's account, would someone else be watching it for signs of activity? A sense of urgency swarmed Ysabel's belly. If someone had been watching the bank, would they be able to follow Anna back to the shelter? Suddenly Jackson's suggestion that Anna might not be safe didn't seem so off-base.

Ysabel sat on the bed beside Anna and laid her hand over the other woman's hand. "The man I work for wants to talk to you about Gregor."

"Who is this man?"

Ysabel inhaled deeply and let it out. "Jackson Champion."

Anna shrank back, pulling her hand free of Ysabel. "The man Gregor worked for?"

"Yes."

"He will kill me for what Gregor did to his ship."

"No, Jackson will not kill you, he wants to help you."

"No, no, he will send me to jail, I will be deported. What will happen to me and Katiya?" She jumped up from the bed and paced the room.

"Anna, what if the men who burned your house down come back again?" She stopped short of saying "to finish the job."

Anna glanced around the room as if looking for her belongings. "I must leave. I go where they cannot find me."

"You don't have any money, Anna. You and your baby need food to live."

"I can't stay here. That man will come. I know it. He will find us."

Ysabel rose from her perch on the bed. "Did you see the man who paid Gregor, Anna?"

She shook her head, tears running down her face. "One time only and he was too far away to see his face. A big man." She raised her hand high above her head and a shiver shook her frame. "A big, bad man."

"He was tall?" Ysabel quelled her excitement. Anna wasn't much over five feet tall. Practically any man would tower over her. Although it wasn't much to go on, it was the most description anyone had reported so far. Anna might be the only person alive who could come close to identifying whoever was responsible for sabotaging Champion Shipping and possibly the Aggie Four Foundation. Which put her in danger. "Anna, if this man thinks you can identify him, he will definitely be looking for you. Mr. Champion can help you hide from him."

She shook her head. "No, no. I can't."

A light tap on the door made Ysabel jump and Anna cry out.

"Anna, a man is on the telephone, asking for an Anna Chernov," Mrs. Rodriguez's voice called out through the wood paneling. "I told him no one by that name lived here. I thought you should know."

Anna grasped Ysabel's hand. "He has found me. He has found me!"

Ysabel held her hands firmly between her own. When the administrator's footsteps faded down the hallway, Ysabel stared into Anna's eyes. "You have to come with me. If he found you here, he'll find you no matter where you run. You don't have the money to help you disappear. Mr. Champion does."

Anna's tears trickled to a stop. "You trust this Mr. Champion?"

Ysabel nodded. "I'd trust him with my life." *Just not my heart.*

Anna took a shaky breath and sighed. "Then I will come with you."

With a nod, Ysabel pulled her cell phone from her pocket. "I'm going to call Mr. Champion now and let him know where we are to pick us up in his truck. You're sure?"

The woman nodded.

A baby wailed in the hallway outside the room. Anna raced for the door and flung it open.

Mrs. Rodriguez carried Katiya toward them, smiling. "She's awake and hungry. That girl's got a set of lungs on her."

Ysabel dialed Jackson's number.

"Everything okay?" he answered, his voice taut.

"Yes." Ysabel glanced at Anna settling on the bed to feed the crying baby.

Anna pulled her shirt up and nestled the baby close to her breast. Like a baby bird eager for her mother's offering, Katiya turned her cheek into her mother's breast, mouth wide open and latched on.

Ysabel's own breasts tingled. Soon she'd be feeding her own baby. What would it feel like to have a baby suckling on her nipples? Her heart filled with longing. Seven months seemed a long time to wait. She wanted to hold her child now.

"I'm headed back for the truck. Don't go anywhere."

"We'll be here." Short of jerking the baby loose from her hold on Anna, they couldn't quite jump up and run down the street without Katiya screaming for her supper. The infant was an effective alarm system to anyone listening or looking for a woman carrying a baby.

Ysabel's toe tapped against the carpet. The sooner they left the shelter the better. If someone knew enough to call here asking for Anna, he might not be far behind. What was keeping Jackson?

Footsteps in the hallway hurried toward Anna's room.

With her breath caught in her throat, Ysabel ran for the door and nearly jumped out of her skin when someone knocked loudly.

"Ms. Chernov, there's a man out here claiming he's here to pick you up." When Ysabel yanked the door open, Mrs. Rodriguez practically fell in. "What should I do?"

"Is he wearing a cowboy hat and driving a pickup?" Ysabel asked.

"Yes, yes, he is. Do you know him?" The older woman's brows knitted into a concerned frown. "We don't like unannounced visitors here. What with this being a battered women's shelter and all."

"It's okay. He's with me and he's okay." Ysabel patted the woman's arm. "Anna, we need to leave."

Anna pressed a finger to her nipple, breaking the baby's suction.

Katiya sucked in a deep, sobbing breath and cried.

Ysabel took the baby into her arms while Anna straightened her clothing and grabbed the diaper bag they'd purchased the previous evening. Everything Anna owned was in that diaper bag. Which didn't amount to much—diapers, two outfits for Katiya and one change of clothing for Anna. That was it.

Ysabel held the whimpering baby against her chest and led the way out to Jackson.

The five or ten minutes Ysabel had been inside the house without him had been the longest of Jackson's life. When she walked toward him carrying an infant, he couldn't keep the smile from curling his lips. "What have you got there?" He leaned close and tickled the baby's chin, the scent of talcum and herbal shampoo mixing to form a not unpleasant combination. He brushed his hand across the baby's soft skin, wishing it was Ysabel's skin he stroked. "Hi, sweetheart. Want to go for a ride?"

Mrs. Rodriguez opened a closet door and tugged an infant's car seat out. "You can take this. I assume you won't be coming back to stay?"

Ysabel looked to Jackson.

He shook his head. They'd take Anna somewhere safe and he'd help her and her child to get a fresh start.

"We won't, Mrs. Rodriguez," Ysabel told the older woman. "But thank you for all your help. We'll return the car seat in a few days."

"Don't worry about it. You can return it anytime."

"Stay here," Jackson told Ysabel and Anna. He left the house first, and spent the next precious few minutes struggling to fit the car seat into the backseat of his pickup. Once he had the straps in place, his gaze panned the street and the nearby houses in both directions. After a long moment, he waved Ysabel and Anna to join him at the truck.

Carrying the baby, Ysabel hustled around the truck and climbed into the backseat. She had the baby strapped in and cinched in seconds. Anna climbed into the seat beside the baby and leaned over to plunk a pacifier in her mouth.

Ysabel dropped down out of the truck and rounded the tailgate, climbing up into the front passenger seat beside Jackson. "Where to?"

He started the engine and set the truck in gear. "The Diamondback Ranch. At least there, you can see your enemy coming from a distance."

Ysabel nodded and settled back in the cab for the hour-long ride in Houston traffic. "Anna said she saw Gregor speak to a big man. She thinks he's the one who ordered Gregor to smuggle the bomb materials and blow up the ship."

Jackson glanced in the rearview mirror at the woman in the backseat. Her pale face and shadowed eyes radiated her fear. "Would you recognize him if you saw him in a picture?"

Anna shrugged and looked down at her baby. "I am not certain. I was hiding and it was dark outside, he stood in the shadows." She yawned and leaned her head back against the seat. "His hair not like Anna's. White."

So the man had pale hair. A big blond man. Jackson wanted to ask more, but Anna's eyes closed.

The woman had to be exhausted, running from a killer and living in fear for her life.

Jackson concentrated on the road, leaving the woman alone. Soon Anna nodded off to sleep.

About that time, Ysabel reached a hand across and touched his leg.

Every nerve ending in that spot and others throughout his body leaped.

"I haven't asked her about talking with Fielding yet. It was all I could do to get her into the truck with you."

"I got that feeling. She's been through a lot."

Ysabel turned in her seat to look over her shoulder. "Do you think she'll be safe at the ranch?"

"Yes, Flint will make sure she's okay. And he'll arrange for her to get a new start someplace when this is all over."

"Good. I'd hate anything bad to happen to her and her baby."

The rest of the ride passed in silence. As they turned off the highway onto the long driveway to the ranch, Ysabel's cell phone rang.

She scrambled in her purse for the device and viewed the screen. "It's Tom," she said as she punched the Talk button. "This is Ysabel."

Jackson alternated checking his position on the road and studying Ysabel's expressions.

Her brows drew together. "You did? A corporation. Did

you find out who it belongs to?" A long pause. "A Houston address. Surely we can track down the owners. That's great, Tom. You're doing a fabulous job. We can look into it more tomorr—Tom?" She glanced across at Jackson. "Tom?"

Her face paled.

Jackson slowed the truck and pulled to the side of the road. "What's happening?"

"I don't know." She pressed the phone to one ear and a hand to the other. "I think he dropped the phone."

A loud banging sound erupted from the cell phone and Ysabel's hand jerked away from her head. "Oh, my God." Her eyes widened and she looked across the console to Jackson. "I think he crashed."

Chapter Thirteen

Her hands shaking, Ysabel called 9-1-1 and reported what she'd heard after Tom dropped his cell phone. Not that she could give them much more information because she didn't know exactly where Tom had been when he wrecked.

Jackson was on the phone and shifting into gear at the same time. Committed to delivering Anna to the ranch, they couldn't turn around until they'd safely delivered her into the care of Flint McKade.

When they reached the ranch, Flint was waiting on the porch with his wife, Lora Leigh.

Even before he'd switched off the engine, Flint was at his truck door, opening it. "I was able to contact the Houston dispatch. They found Tom's vehicle in a ditch off Interstate 45."

Ysabel climbed out of the pickup and rounded the hood to stand in front of Flint. "How is he?"

Lora Leigh joined Flint. "Still alive from what the dispatcher could tell us. They're having to cut him out of his car."

"Damn it!" Jackson slammed his palm against the steering wheel. "What the hell happened?"

"According to one of the police officers, someone ran him off the road on his way home from work," Flint said. "Witnesses say it was deliberate."

"Poor Tom." Ysabel's hand hovered over her belly, plucking at her shirt. "I can't believe someone would attack in broad daylight."

"Did anyone get a make on the car?" Jackson asked.

"A witness reported a dark-blue Saturn, a rental car. They were able to get a partial on the license. Special Agent Fielding is checking into it."

"Good." Jackson climbed down from the truck and opened the door for Anna, whose face had paled considerably at the news. "Could you take care of Ms. Chernov? I need to get back to town."

"You bet." Lora Leigh climbed inside and unsnapped the safety belts holding the baby and the car seat. "Come, Anna, I'll show you your room. And don't worry, Flint has a state-of-the-art security system inside the house. You'll be safe here."

"If there's anything more I can do, let me know." Flint held out a hand to Jackson and the men shook.

"There is one thing," Jackson said. "See if you can talk Anna into a meeting with Special Agent Fielding. Maybe he can arrange for a composite sketch of the man she saw with her husband."

Anna hesitated, her eyes wide. "No, I cannot risk it."

Jackson sighed. "Just hear what Flint has to say. We won't force you to do anything you don't want to do."

Anna's gaze met Jackson's. After a moment, she nodded. "I will listen."

Ysabel gave her a hug. "You'll be okay. Lora Leigh is a sweetheart. She'll help you with Katiya."

"Absolutely. We were able to borrow a crib from one of the ranch hands. Come see." Lora Leigh, carrying the car seat with the sleeping baby inside, led Anna into the house.

Ysabel climbed into the truck, her stomach churning, the awful acids burning for release.

Jackson slid into the driver's seat, his gaze on her as he started the engine. "Are you okay?"

"No. I'm not." Tears welled in her eyes, but she held on to them until Jackson turned the truck back toward Houston. "I shouldn't have involved Tom in this."

"Ysabel, you don't know if Tom's accident was due to the hacking he's been doing."

"Why else would someone deliberately run him off the road?" Anger surged through her. Deep down, she knew she wasn't angry at Jackson, but he was there and she had to lash out at someone or something. "What have we accomplished so far? Nothing!" She slammed her hand on the arm rest. "Nothing but a burned-down house, two dead terrorists and a kid on his way to the hospital. We're not exactly batting a thousand here. What are you going to do about it? How are you going to make it stop?"

Jackson's lips tightened into a thin line. "I don't know. But you're right. It's not fair that Tom, Anna and you got caught up in all this. I don't know what I can do to make the attacks stop, but I can do something about you and Tom. You're not to work on this anymore. In fact, as of today, your resignation is official. That way you're not involved with Champion Shipping at all."

Ysabel's anger shriveled up and died at his words, replaced by an ominous sense of dread. This was it. She'd finally gotten what she wanted. Then why didn't she feel better about it? When she should be relieved, she could think only about the emptiness of spending the rest of her life without ever seeing Jackson again. No more poking fun, arguing politics and comparing notes on how to improve Champion Shipping.

"Okay," she managed to say. Her hands clasped together in her lap, pressed over her belly. When she should be planning her next steps, her move and her job search, all she could do was sit and stare out the window, her mind a complete blank.

Jackson sat stone-cold silent in the seat beside her all the way back to the outskirts of Houston. As he maneuvered through the late-afternoon traffic, his cell phone rang. Flint called to give him the name of the hospital they'd taken Tom to.

"I can drop you at the office or take you with me to see Tom," Jackson offered.

"Tom," she said.

At the hospital, Ysabel questioned the volunteer at the information desk who located Tom's room in intensive care. At first, the nurses wouldn't let them in to see Tom because neither one of them was a family member. Ysabel tried to explain that Tom's family lived in Lubbock and they couldn't get there until late that night, but the nurses held firm.

Jackson took over. One call to the administrator and a reminder of how much money Champion Shipping contributed annually to the hospital and they were ushered into Tom's room.

Tom lay amidst an array of machines, wires and tubes. His young face bruised and lacerated, the dark smudges a sharp contrast against the crisp white sheets.

"We just gave him a sedative, so he won't be able to talk long, if at all," the nurse informed them, in a hushed voice.

"Hey, Tom." Ysabel lifted the young man's hand in hers, careful not to touch anything broken or bruised. A knot rose to her throat as she stared down into his battered face.

Tom's eyelids flickered open. "Did I die? Are you an angel?" His cracked lips turned up in a wry smile. He winced and the smile disappeared. "Guess I won't be smiling anytime soon," he croaked in a voice barely above a whisper.

Jackson rounded the bed to the other side and shook his

head. "And I thought I had the corner on the dare-devil driving. You sure know how to make an impression on the boss."

"Does this mean I get a raise?" Tom chuckled and coughed.

Jackson smiled down at the kid. "We'll talk about it."

Ysabel's heart swelled at the tenderness in Jackson's voice. He really was good to his employees. She'd never had a complaint. Hopefully, she'd find a new boss as considerate. A sob rose in her throat.

The younger man's eyes drifted closed. "Ysabel, could you tell the boss I'll be late for work tomorrow?"

Ysabel swallowed the lump in her throat and she gently squeezed his hand. "Don't worry. I'm sure the boss will let it slide this once."

"Not so sure. 'Specially because his girl is holding my hand." Tom's breathing evened out and his face went slack.

Ysabel's cheeks heated. Tom didn't realize how far from the truth his words were. The boss's girl. Ha! He'd just accepted her resignation, effectively cutting her out of his life forever.

The nurse appeared in the doorway. "You'll have to leave now. Mr. Walker needs rest."

In the elevator going down, Jackson spoke first. "I don't feel comfortable leaving Tom here without protection."

"I could stay with him."

Jackson shook his head. "No. You're exhausted, you need to get home. Not to mention, you've had your share of near misses." He flipped his phone open. "It's time to hire some help."

While Jackson called around for a bodyguard for hire, Ysabel did some calling of her own to her sister Delia.

Twenty minutes later, Jackson shut his phone and scrubbed a hand over his face. "I have a man on the way.

Once he gets here, we can go."

Delia chose that moment to hurry into the lobby of the hospital.

Ysabel faced Jackson. "I have my own transportation. If it's all right by you, I'll collect my things from the office tonight."

Jackson felt like he'd been sucker-punched in the gut. Oh yeah, he'd accepted her resignation. What the hell was he thinking? Had he really said she could leave? If Ysabel left, he'd have no way to protect her from whoever was trying to kill her. Panic seized him. "About that. I didn't mean it. I still want you to stay on for the full two weeks."

Ysabel smiled sadly. "You can't take it back, Jackson. You verbally accepted my resignation. That's as binding as a signed contract."

"But it's not in writing. It would be your word against mine. I could take you to court and keep you from leaving before the end of your two-week notice."

She shook her head. "Jackson Champion, you're a man of your word. You wouldn't lie in court to save your life. Just let me go. I'll be okay and so will you."

Jackson wasn't so sure. If he let Ysabel walk out of his life now, he'd never see her again. "If it's a matter of pay, I'll double your salary."

Her brows dipped. For a brilliant businessman, Jackson Champion could be clueless when it came to people. No, when it came to her. "It's never been about the pay, Jackson."

"Then why quit now?"

"I have to. That's all there is to it."

"Is it because of what's happened between us? I'll leave you alone, if that's what you want."

"No. Maybe someday I'll tell you. But for now, I can't." Her voice choked on the last words.

Her sister stepped up beside her and jabbed her elbow into Ysabel's arm. "Tell him."

Ysabel glared at her sister. "No. Not now."

"If you don't, I will."

Ysabel grabbed her sister's arm and jerked her toward the door. "Goodbye, Jackson. Come on, Delia. I don't need another conscience."

The two women hurried away, leaving Jackson standing alone in the lobby. She was leaving. Damn it! Ysabel was leaving and all the money he owned couldn't stop her.

Money hadn't changed her mind, not that he really expected it to. Ysabel wasn't driven to make millions like he was. For the first time since he'd known Ysabel he wondered just what did motivate her. She was always talking about her family. Obviously family meant a lot to her. She loved her family and hoped to have one of her own someday. Hadn't she told him that once upon a time?

Jackson's own family had abandoned him to the foster-care system, a system that hadn't been the ideal place for a child to learn what families were all about. He'd been shuffled from one home to another. What did he know about how a family worked?

Ysabel knew. Her large, extended family was spread out across Houston and south Texas, but they were close like a family was supposed to be.

Was that it? Did she want a chance for a family of her own? Did she want to leave him so she'd have time to date and find a man to love her like she deserved? Searing heat burned in his chest at the thought of another man holding Ysabel in his arms, making love to her sweet body, giving her children. Was he jealous? When Jenna had ditched him for an old boyfriend, he hadn't felt as though he couldn't breathe, or like he wanted to smash a man's face, or as if he couldn't live to the next day.

Jackson Champion had never been jealous before and he

wasn't sure he was now. But whatever he was feeling, he didn't like it.

If she was leaving to take the time to date and find a man to love her, could he convince her to stay if he told her that *he* loved her? Would that make a difference?

Ysabel had told him he was a man of his word. Could he tell her he loved her and mean it? Did he love her?

The question rammed him like a wrecker ball. Did he love Ysabel?

"Sir? Are you Jackson Champion?" A bulked-out man dressed in a tight black polo shirt and black trousers stopped in front of him, removing mirrored aviator glasses.

Jackson focused on the man, realizing for the first time since Ysabel had walked away that he was still standing in the lobby of the hospital.

"I'm Toby Layne. The agency sent me over. I'm your new bodyguard." He cracked his knuckles and flexed his muscles. "Whose body do you want me to guard?"

DELIA was waiting for her outside her apartment when Ysabel returned from the office, carrying a box with the personal items she'd unloaded from her desk. Although the box was heavy, the contents didn't amount to much—a few pictures, her framed college diplomas and her favorite stapler.

She and Delia had spent two hours on a hot dealership lot, choosing a car Ysabel couldn't have cared less about. She didn't have the heart to tell the salesman her only requirement was an affordable payment for a woman working for minimum wage. She'd cash in some of her 401K. That and her insurance payoff would equal a sizable down payment to keep her monthly outgo reasonable.

After promising her life away, Ysabel drove off the lot in a sedate four-door charcoal gray sedan any soccer mom would be proud of.

"Didn't I just see you an hour ago?" She balanced the box on her hip and fished in her purse with her spare hand. "What are you doing here? Don't you have a party to go to or whatever single girls do today?"

"Not until the weekend, *mi hermana*. I have a few minutes I can spend helping my pregnant sister leave the man she loves. Give me that." She reached for the box and held it while Ysabel unlocked the door.

Part of Ysabel wanted to be left alone to sort through the box and what was left of her life. The other part couldn't stand the thought of sitting by herself in her apartment, the four walls closing in around her. "Come in then. I could use some diversion."

Before she'd closed the door firmly, Delia started, "Why didn't you tell him?"

"If you're going to nag, just turn around and leave right now."

Delia set the box on the coffee table and raised her hands in surrender. "Okay, okay, I promise not to nag you about telling Jackson you're pregnant with *his* child."

"Good, because I really don't think I could take it right now." Ysabel choked back a sob, but she couldn't stop the rush of tears to her eyes. "I can't believe I'll never see him again."

"Oh, you'll see him all right." Delia wandered toward the kitchen and opened the refrigerator. "In court most likely. Girl, you don't have any food in your refrigerator. What are you feeding that baby?"

"I don't know." Ysabel flopped onto the brushed leather sofa and plopped her feet next to a box.

"Well, you can't starve yourself without starving your baby. I'm calling out for Chinese."

While Delia placed the order, Ysabel pressed her fingers

to her eyes, trying unsuccessfully to stem the flow of tears. "What is wrong with me? I never cry!"

Delia set the phone on the counter and hurried to sit beside Ysabel on the sofa. "You're pregnant. You're going to cry. Get used to it."

"Since when are you an expert on pregnant women?"

"Don't you remember? I stayed with our cousin Carmen during her last two months before José decided to appear. She taught me everything I need to know about babies." Delia raised her hand. "I do so solemnly swear I'll never have any of my own." Her face wrinkled in a horrified grimace. "How anyone could want to have children is beyond me. All that blood, screaming and pain."

"Thanks." Ysabel stared at her sister, without lifting her head from the back of the sofa. "I'll remember to bring you with me when I need a root canal. Nothing like telling it like it is to make a girl scared to death."

Her sister had the grace to blush. "Sorry. Now is not a good time to tell you all that."

"No, duh."

"The point was, you're pregnant, your hormones are whacky, you just said goodbye to the man you love. What's not to cry about?" Delia wrapped her in her arms and hugged her. "You go right ahead and cry. You deserve to."

Ysabel chuckled and hiccupped, pushing her sister away. "Thanks, but I need to get past this."

"You won't until you tell Jackson that he has a baby on the way."

Ysabel leaned her head back again, her head aching. "I know."

"Until you do, you won't be able to get on with your life. And it's not fair to run away before you do it. Jackson has the right to know where you and the baby are. He's the father."

"You promised not to nag." Ysabel laid her arm over her face.

"I know, I just feel so strongly about this and deep down, I know you do too. Your sense of fairness won't let you rest until you tell him."

"You're right." Ysabel sat up. "I can't think past that time. I should have told him as soon as I found out."

"Now you're talking."

Ysabel stood and straightened her pants suit. "Question is how?"

"How what?"

"How do I tell him?" Her head throbbed, her stomach knotting at the prospect of telling Jackson he was going to be a father. What man liked being broadsided by an admission like that? How would he take it? Would he be angry, disappointed, shocked?

"Why don't you try the straight and simple? 'Jackson, I'm having your baby.'"

Ysabel tapped a finger to her lips and stared out of her window at the lights of downtown Houston. Her apartment wasn't in the penthouse, but she had a good view of the rest of the city. She could see the light from Jackson's penthouse, albeit from a distance. Not that she could tell whether he was home. She'd left him at the hospital three hours ago. Would he be home?

Now that she wasn't working for him anymore, she might as well get it over with. He might be too distracted by what was happening with Champion Shipping to be concerned about her and a baby. "Okay, I'm going to tell him." Her decision made, she marched to the counter where she'd left her purse and slipped her cell phone from a side pocket.

Delia squealed. "You are *not* going to tell him over the phone, are you?"

Ysabel's finger hovered over the speed dial for Jackson's cell number. "Why not?"

"*Madre de Dios!* You can't tell a man he's going to be a father over the phone." She practically leaped at Ysabel, grabbing her phone. "You have to tell him in person."

Her heart hammered against her ribs. "No way. I can't." Even as she said the words, she knew that was exactly what she had to do.

"You have to." Delia slipped an arm around Ysabel's waist and pulled her against her side. "You know he deserves that much."

Ysabel huffed out a sigh. "I hate it when you're right." She stole the phone from her sister's hands and tossed it into her purse. "Then I'll go to his place right now and tell him. That way I can leave when I want to. If he comes here, I'd have a harder time getting him to leave."

"Good thinking." Delia smiled. Was there a little devilish gleam in her green eyes so much like Ysabel's? "Go on, *mi hermana.* I'll wait here in case you need someone to talk to when you get back."

"You'd do that for me?" Ysabel's eyes pooled again with her ready tears.

"Of course. I'm not leaving until that Chinese food gets here." She laughed, turning Ysabel toward the door. "Hurry up before it gets any later. It's already after nine."

"I'm going." Ysabel's feet dragged toward the door, every step bringing her closer to her last face-to-face with the only man she'd ever loved. Foolishly, yes, but loved nonetheless. "It takes only about fifteen minutes there, fifteen minutes back and a few minutes to break the news to him. I'll be back in less than an hour. Keep my food warm." Not that she'd want to touch it after telling Jackson the news. Right at that moment, she wanted to throw up and she didn't expect that feeling to go away even after she told him.

On the ride down the elevator and the walk out to her car, Ysabel told herself everything would be all right.

When she arrived at Jackson's building and entered the parking garage, her throat closed up and she fought to breathe normally. She hoped like hell telling Jackson wasn't going to be the biggest mistake of her life.

A frown pulled at her brow. Jackson's car wasn't in his assigned spot.

Why hadn't she thought to call him before she came over? She pulled her phone from her purse. Before she could place the call, a loud knock on her window made her scream and drop her phone.

Her pulse jumping, Ysabel starred out at Jenna Nilsson.

"Ysabel, help me, please," she cried. Her pretty face was bruised, her lip cracked and bleeding.

Ysabel shoved her car into park and jumped out. "Jenna, what happened?"

"It's my brother," she sobbed, her words garbled through the tears. "He's gone crazy."

"Your brother?" Ysabel hadn't known Jenna had a brother. She'd assumed she was an only child. Nothing in any of her conversations with the woman had indicated otherwise. She wrapped the girl in her arms and patted her back. "Take a deep breath and tell me about it."

"No, we can't stay here." She stared around the parking garage, her eyes wide, her hands shaking. "He'll find me and kill me."

"Then get in my car. I'll take you to the police station."

"No!" Jenna pulled free of her hold and stepped back, her head shaking back and forth. "No. You can't go to the police. He'll find me."

"But the police will help."

"No, you can't, because he's—" she dropped to her knees

and buried her face in her hands. "He's—" More sobs muffled her words.

Ysabel squatted down beside Jenna. "Because he's what?"

"Because he *is* a cop," a deep, familiar voice said, before something hard and cold pressed against Ysabel's back. "Don't turn around, don't move."

Jenna shrank away from Ysabel's captor. "Oh, God. No. Brody, you can't do this. You can't."

"Shut up!" the man said.

Ysabel's entire body shook at the realization that the man with a gun pointed at her back was a member of the sheriff's department. The detective investigating the bombing case, Brody Green. "He's your brother?" she asked Jenna.

"My stepbrother. You have to stop him. He's planning to blow up—"

"I said shut up!" Brody stepped forward and slammed the barrel of the pistol against Jenna's cheekbone. She crumpled to the ground without even a whimper.

Ysabel moved toward the unconscious woman. Before she could reach her, a hand grabbed her hair and yanked her back. "Leave her."

"But she needs medical attention."

"Let her die. She's of no use to me now. She never could get it right."

"What do you mean?"

"She was supposed to marry Jackson Champion. If she had, none of this would have gotten out of hand." He jerked her toward his car. "Now get in."

Chapter Fourteen

After checking over the bodyguard's credentials and briefing him on his duties, Jackson left the hospital, a full hour after Ysabel. Once in his truck, he drove around the city in a complete mental fog. For the first time in his life, he didn't know exactly what he needed to do. Ysabel had been the rock in his world, the one who kept him on track. Even during his two-month absence, he was comforted by the knowledge that she was back home, running the office, smoothing his path. There for him.

Too jittery to go home, he jumped when his cell phone rang, disappointment filling him when the number came up Unknown. To him that meant not Ysabel.

For a moment he let it ring. But the chance it might be news on who had attacked Tom made him reach for the hands-free button on the dash. "Jackson speaking."

"Mr. Champion, this is Special Agent Fielding. I realize it's late, but is there a possibility you could stop by our field office off Interstate 610?"

"What do you have?"

"We have the identity of who rented the vehicle that ran Tom off the road."

"I'll be there in ten minutes." Jackson turned onto Interstate 10 and floored the accelerator. Finally, a clue. Eight and a half minutes later, he skidded to a stop in the parking lot at the Houston field office of the Federal Bureau of Investigations on T. C. Jester Boulevard.

Fielding met him at the front door and led him through the maze of offices to a conference room set up with a computer and a large white board. On the board was the time line of the chain of events going back to when one of Champion Shipping's airplanes exploded on the tarmac carrying a shipment of Arabians for Flint and Akeem several months ago.

"Take a seat," the agent invited.

Jackson dropped into a padded chair, staring around at the room and its contents. "You guys have been busy."

"Yeah, but this might be the first real clue we've gotten in regards to the potential terrorist plot we think might be underfoot right here in Houston."

Jackson nodded, his gut clenching at the thought. Houston was anything but prepared for a terrorist attack. With over a million people in Houston proper, an attack would be devastating. "I know my ships might have been involved in transporting dirty bomb-making materials. I've tightened security and run another background check on all my employees working in and around the shipyards."

"Good. That will help. But we think the damage may already be done and dirty bomb materials are already here in the city. We just don't know where and when they'll strike."

"So what did you find?"

"The vehicle that ran Tom off the road earlier was a rental car, leased out to a J. Nilsson."

"Jenna?" Jackson sat back. "You think Jenna is capable of running a man off the road?"

"Anyone is capable of running another person off the road just by not paying attention. But no." Fielding shook his head. "Witnesses said the driver was a man. So we ran a check on your ex-fiancée. And you'll never believe what we found."

Jackson leaned forward.

"Jenna's half brother is none other than the sheriff department's Detective Brody Green."

Jackson scrubbed a hand over his face. "Why didn't I know that?"

"Did you run a background check on Miss Nilsson?"

"Yes." He'd had Ysabel schedule the background check after their first date.

"I'm betting Pinkerton didn't go any further than her mother and father. You see, her mother had a baby when she was a teenager, Brody. She gave him to his father to raise. It wasn't until Jenna's mother died in a car accident that she found out she had a brother."

Jackson crossed his arms over his chest. "So, her brother is a detective. You think he's the one who ran Tom off the road?"

"We dusted the car for prints and found nothing. He must have used gloves while driving. But he didn't use them when he filled the gas tank. We were able to lift a clean print and run it through our databases. We got a match on our detective."

"But why would he want to sabotage the investigation?"

"Could have something to do with that debt he's accumulated at the casinos in Biloxi, Mississippi." Fielding smiled grimly. "Remember, he's in over his head to the tune of three hundred thousand dollars."

To Jackson, three hundred thousand dollars wasn't that much these days. But on a detective's salary…

"Have you brought him in for questioning?"

"That's the problem, we can't find him. He didn't show up for work today and didn't call in."

"Great, the man's a potential menace and no one knows where he is?" The conversation he'd had with Detective Green played back in his mind. "Green doesn't like me."

"Yeah, I gathered as much. Do you think it had anything to do with your relationship with Jenna?"

"Now that I know he's her half-brother, I'd bet my fortune on it." Jackson tried to recall his exact wording. "He said something about SOBs like me making promises they never intended to keep and then backing out without care for the repercussions. He said, it would come back to haunt me someday."

"Do you think he's the one sabotaging Champion Shipping and the Aggie Four Foundation?" Fielding asked.

"I didn't get the impression he was smart enough to orchestrate anything that difficult. He's mad at me about something, but I'm not sure what." Jackson dug through his memory to think of what and all he had was his relationship to Jenna.

"Do you think he was counting on your marrying Jenna so that he could get his hands on some of your money to pay back his debts?"

Jackson chewed on that thought. "If he wanted me to marry Jenna so that he could get his hands on the money, why would he try to sabotage my corporation?"

"I don't know." Fielding tapped a pen to the table top. "You say Miss Sanchez has been targeted on several occasions?"

"Yes."

"Do you think he feels like she's a threat to you and Jenna patching things up?"

The recent image of Jenna in his office practically throwing herself at him sprang to mind. "Jenna tried to get me to take her back." He looked up at Fielding without seeing him. "If he thinks Jenna and I are getting back together, he doesn't know that it was Jenna who called off the wedding, not me. She's in love with another man."

"Maybe she's afraid of Green. Afraid he'll hurt her if she doesn't marry you. Maybe he thinks you dumped his sister for Miss Sanchez." Fielding grinned. "The chemistry between the two of you is pretty obvious even to a stranger like me."

Jackson stood up so fast, his chair shot out behind him, tipping over to crash against the tiled floor. "If Jenna hasn't told him the truth, he might keep trying until he succeeds in getting Ysabel permanently out of the picture. I have to go."

"Before you go, what did Tom find that could have Detective Green scared enough to run him off the road?"

Jackson paused in the doorframe. "He hacked into the Cayman bank account that transferred money into Gregor Volsky's account. He was able to trace the account back to a corporation here in Houston."

Fielding's brows rose. "Any idea which one?"

"None. We'll have to wait for Tom to come out of the sedative they've got him on. But you're welcome to the computer he used in my office."

"We're working on a warrant to search Green's home and office. Should have that soon."

"Great. Now if you'll excuse me, I need to check on Ysabel."

"Right. Do you want me to send an agent to her apartment?"

"No, I'll be there before any agent can be mobilized."

Fielding grinned. "She's a keeper, your Miss Sanchez."

Jackson nodded. "I know." He only wished he was keeping her. He'd practically kicked her out of his life by accepting her resignation. If he'd been in his right mind, he would have used the time he had left to convince her to stay.

The nights they'd spent in each others' arms had been pure ecstasy. Ysabel had been every bit as passionate as he had. But she'd never said anything about love.

Was love a factor in their relationship? He thought back over the years with Ysabel by his side at Champion Shipping. Her wit, humor and intelligence made him smile, kept him on his toes. He thought of all the women he'd paraded past her and her continued good attitude, if not a few sarcastic remarks about their IQ or lack thereof.

He couldn't think of life without her. If that was love…

Once outside the FBI building, he pulled out his cell phone and dialed Ysabel's number. After the fourth ring, her voice mail message played. "Ysabel, meet me at your place. It's important that we talk. Don't go out, don't open your door for anyone, including and especially Detective Green." He clicked the Off button and pressed harder on the accelerator. Why wasn't she answering? Was it because his number showed on the display? "Jesus, Ysabel, now's not the time to ignore me. Pick up the phone. Call me," Jackson said out loud.

He had to get to her before that lunatic Green did. Within minutes, he slammed his truck to a stop outside Ysabel's apartment building, threw it in Park and leaped down. The ride up the elevator, all fourteen floors, nearly killed him. Taking the stairs might have been faster. All the way up, he couldn't help the overwhelming sense of dread washing over him. What if she wasn't there? What if Green had gotten to her first?

The elevator door dinged and before the doors fully opened, Jackson squeezed through and raced down the hall to her apartment, banging on the door. "Ysabel!"

"Keep your shirt on," a voice called out from within.

Relief washed over Jackson. She was home. All that worrying for nothing.

When the door opened, it took him a moment to realize the person in front of him wasn't Ysabel. She looked like her, but she wasn't Ysabel. Delia.

Jackson pushed past her. "Where's Ysabel?" He strode through the apartment, his chest tightening with each step.

"Hello to you, too." Delia leaned in the doorway, a smile curling her lips. "My sister is on her way to your place. She had something important to say to you that couldn't wait."

"She shouldn't be running around the city at night. What's so important it couldn't have waited until morning?" Jackson returned to the door, wanting to shake someone for answers.

"I'm not at liberty to say. You'll have to ask her. She left fifteen minutes ago. She should be at your apartment about now." Delia stepped aside. "If you hurry, you might catch her."

"If she shows up before I find her, tell her to call me and stay put." Jackson hurried through the door and loped down the hallway to the elevator.

"Will do, big daddy." Delia called out behind him in a soft voice he almost didn't hear.

Once in his truck, he performed a U-turn and sped along the street toward his downtown apartment. He hoped he'd catch her before she left his building. Hell, he hoped he'd catch her before Green did.

YSABEL struggled to sit up in the backseat of Detective Green's unmarked sheriff's deputy sedan. The hard plastic zip strap cinching her wrists together behind her back wasn't helping her gain her balance. Jenna lay unconscious on the floorboard in front of her—at least Ysabel *hoped* she was only unconscious. She swallowed hard on the lump of fear threatening to choke off her air. Somehow she had to get out of this situation. Her baby deserved a chance to live. "Where are you taking me?" she asked the back of the man's head.

Green didn't answer, but the speed of the vehicle increased and the sound of the pavement smoothed as if he'd gained access to a freeway.

"Mr. Champion will be looking for me and the FBI is on to you. You know you're not going to get away with anything," Ysabel lied, hopefully.

"Shut up, you stupid woman. The FBI knows nothing.

They think a bunch of foreigners are responsible for what's been going on and as far as I'm concerned, they can keep on thinking that. They'll never suspect me."

"You're wrong," she argued, just to keep him talking. Maybe if she made him angry enough, he'd stop the car and get out. With her hands bound behind her back, she couldn't reach a door handle and she didn't know whether the doors had to be opened from the outside like most police cars.

"Detective Green, Jenna needs a doctor."

"Not where you two are going."

Dread filled Ysabel's empty stomach.

"Besides, it's her own fault. If she hadn't screwed up her wedding with that jerk, Champion, none of this would have happened."

"What did Jenna's wedding to Jackson have to do with kidnapping me?" Try as she might, she couldn't make the connection.

"Doesn't matter now—and it will matter even less when it's all said and done."

Ysabel took a deep breath and asked, "What do you mean when all's said and done?"

"I'm going to blow Houston off the map." Green laughed, sending a cold slither of fear washing over Ysabel's skin.

"You were the one importing all the bomb-making materials?" Ysabel asked.

"No, and that's the beauty of it. They'll never link me to that because I wasn't the one who had the stuff smuggled into America. The only people who know I'm involved are in this car and after today, you two won't be blabbing."

Because he planned on blowing them up with the rest of Houston. Ysabel didn't have to be a mind-reader to figure that one out, but she'd be damned if she let it happen. Her baby depended on her to use her brain and get herself and Jenna out of this alive.

"Why? You're a cop, sworn to protect the people of Houston. Why would you want to destroy the city?"

"Why do you think?"

"Someone made you mad?" she guessed, completely at a loss for a reason good enough to destroy so many lives.

"That's only part of it. Let's just say someone made me an offer I couldn't refuse."

Ysabel gasped. "You're doing this for money?"

"Hell, yeah. The Rasnovian dissidents would have done it for nothing, just to make a point and an example out of the Americans. I'm not that idealistic." He snorted. "Cold hard cash motivates me."

"That means one other person knows about your involvement besides Jenna and me. Aren't you afraid he'll get caught and take you down with you?"

"No way. He has more money than God. Enough to make sure he's never found out."

"Don't you know that bad guys never win?"

"Lady, when you've worked with the kind of criminals I've worked with for more years than I care to admit, you'd realize how wrong that statement is. The criminals are rarely caught. The bad guys are getting away with murder."

Ysabel wiggled her hands in the plastic strap. Unless she could find something to rub it against and break it, she wasn't getting loose from the thin, hard bond. She stared down at Jenna, wishing she could reach her to check for a pulse. The poor woman had a bruise the size of a baseball on her cheekbone and her eye was almost swelled shut. "Jenna," she whispered, scooting across the seat to lean over her.

Detective Green swerved, sending Ysabel rolling forward on top of Jenna.

She struggled to right herself, inch by inch, scooting her butt back up onto the backseat. When she looked down at Jenna, the woman's eyes blinked open.

Ysabel let out the breath she'd been holding. "Jenna, wake up, you have to help me."

Jenna's clouded eyes cleared and widened. She would have sat bolt upright if Ysabel didn't choose that time to roll back on top of her to keep her down.

"Shh, don't let him know you're conscious," Ysabel whispered directly into Jenna's ear, hoping the sound of the car engine and tires on the pavement kept Green from hearing her words. "Nod if you understand."

Jenna nodded, sucking in a labored breath. She couldn't breathe with Ysabel on top of her.

As quickly as she could, Ysabel scooted back up on the seat. "Why involve Jenna in your scheme? What has she done to deserve to die?"

"What do you care? She was in your way of marrying your rich boss."

"That isn't true." Ysabel stared down at Jenna, all the envy she'd felt for the other woman gone. She knew the reason Jenna had called off the wedding. She'd gone back to her ex-boyfriend. What she didn't understand was her desperate attempt to patch things up with Jackson after two months. "What did you mean if Jenna had married Jackson none of this would have happened?"

Detective Green snorted. "I would have gotten the money from her, instead of doing it the hard way."

"You think Jackson would have given you money through Jenna?" She snorted. "You obviously don't know Jackson Champion. So now you're being paid as a mercenary?"

"That's right."

"All for money?"

"When you don't have it and someone wants it from you, you'll do just about anything."

An icy shiver raked Ysabel's skin. "Including murder?"

"Babe, someone's gonna die and it ain't gonna be me."

Chapter Fifteen

Jackson's truck tires squealed as he rounded the corners into the parking garage beneath the downtown building where he lived. When he veered around the concrete column leading to his private parking space, he slammed on the brakes.

A brand new car stood blocking his space, the door wide open with no one inside. The car had to be Ysabel's.

Damn. Green had gotten to her.

Jackson whipped out his cell phone and punched the speed dial number for Special Agent Fielding.

After only one ring, the agent answered. "Fielding speaking."

"He's got her," Jackson said, his voice catching. He cleared his throat and tried again. "I think Detective Green has Ysabel." He explained what he'd found, ending with, "We have to find her before…"

"We'll find her, Jackson. Don't you worry."

"How? I have no idea where he would have taken her."

"We have a GPS tracking device planted on his work car and his home car. If he's out driving somewhere, we'll find him. Let me get my guys working on it. I'll get back with you as soon as I know anything. Don't do anything until you hear from me."

Jackson hit the Off button and sat staring at Ysabel's car. Don't do anything? Was the agent nuts? How could he just sit back and wait for something to happen? That something could be the death of the only woman he'd dared to love. He sat back against his plush leather seat, his stomach in knots, his head spinning with the realization he loved a woman. No. He loved Ysabel.

Now that he recognized how he felt, he wouldn't rest until he told her. If he got the chance.

Jackson slipped his shift into Reverse and turned his truck. He couldn't wait to go looking for her. He had to find her himself. As he drove out of the parking garage, he dialed Flint and Akeem on conference call.

"I need your help," he started without an introduction or anything.

"What's happening?"

Jackson filled them in on Ysabel's abduction and who he thought it might be.

"We're on our way," Flint said.

"I'm getting into my truck as we speak," Akeem added. "In the meantime, doesn't Ysabel have a cousin in the sheriff's department? Contact him and see what he can do."

"I will." Out of habit and with no real direction to turn, Jackson headed toward the Port of Houston. Once on the freeway, he dialed 9-1-1. When the dispatcher answered, he barked, "I have an emergency and need to speak with Mitch Stanford in the sheriff's department, immediately."

"Sir, is this a life-or-death emergency? Perhaps we can help you."

"This is Jackson Champion of Champion Shipping. This call is a matter of life and death. It's imperative I speak with Mitch Stanford and only Mr. Stanford. Now, please find him."

The woman put him on hold, piping Muzak into his ear. After two of the longest minutes of his life, the line clicked.

"Stanford speaking. What do you have, Mr. Champion?"

Jackson told Mitch everything he knew thus far.

"You think Green has Ysabel?" Stanford asked.

"I don't have anything but her empty car to go on, but my gut tells me yes."

"He didn't show up for work today and he hasn't called to report in. I'll get our people on it right away."

"Thanks." Jackson clicked the Off button and stared straight ahead. Where would the man take her?

His cell phone buzzed and he flipped it open. "Jackson."

"We've got a location on Green's work car."

"Where is it?"

"Headed east on Pasadena Freeway toward the Port of Houston." Agent Fielding paused. "Mr. Champion, you should let the FBI and the police handle this."

"He has Ysabel," Jackson said through clenched teeth, his fingers practically crushing the phone in his hand. Already headed that direction, he slammed his foot to the floor, closed his phone and dropped it into the cup holder.

DETECTIVE Green drove, oblivious to the life-or-death struggle in the backseat of his sedan.

Ysabel turned her back to Jenna and scooted up far enough that the other woman could reach the plastic zip tie holding her wrists together.

Jenna tugged at it while Ysabel kept Green engaged in conversation to cover any sounds they might make.

"Why do you hate Jackson Champion so much?" Ysabel asked.

"He's just like all the fat rich men who walk all over the little guys. They never seem to have enough money, just take, take, take. Well, I plan to give him a little more than he bargained for."

"What did he do to you personally?"

"He didn't marry my stupid little sister like he was supposed to. He was too good for her."

"Why do you care? You weren't marrying Jackson."

"No, but her marriage meant money to me."

"Just because she married Jackson didn't mean she'd have access to all of his money."

"She damned well better have. I told the stupid bitch not to sign any prenuptial agreements. We made a deal. I'd keep her ex-boyfriend out of jail on drug charges and she'd pay off a few debts for me."

"Debts?" Ysabel asked.

Jenna pulled Ysabel's hair until her head was close enough that she could whisper, "Three hundred thousand in gambling debt, my brother didn't know when to quit."

"None of your damned business! She owed me for saving her stupid boyfriend." He gunned the accelerator and the car fishtailed, sliding off the road into gravel. "It's showtime."

He stopped the car and got out.

"I'm sorry, Ysabel, I couldn't loosen it," Jenna called softly.

Fearing Green meant to shoot them here and now, Ysabel aimed her feet at the door as it opened. "Be ready, Jenna. When I say go, get out and run as fast as you can."

"But I can't leave you."

"Yes, you can and will. Just do it," she hissed.

The door jerked open and Brody Green leaned in. "Come on, we have alternate transportation."

Ysabel cocked her legs and kicked out as hard as she could, catching Brody in the jaw.

The surprise attack sent him staggering backward. He slipped in the gravel and fell.

"Go, Jenna, go!"

Jenna rolled out of the car and struggled to her feet.

Before she could get two yards from the car, Green was up and onto her, grabbing her around the middle. Although she kicked and screamed, he held tight.

As soon as Jenna left the car, Ysabel had scooted to the edge of the seat. Now she leaned forward and propelled herself out of the car and ran toward Green, head down like a charging bull.

She caught him in the middle of his back, aiming for his kidney.

He grunted, his grip loosening on Jenna. She dropped to the ground and rolled to the side, kicking at his ankles to get away. She crab-walked backward, scuffling in the gravel, but slipping too much to get her feet under her.

Green kicked her in the side. A sharp snap sounded clearly in the night sky and Jenna doubled over, clutching her rib-cage. "Oh, God," she wheezed.

Ysabel's head hurt from hitting Brody so hard that she barely managed to remain upright. It took her too long to right herself. By the time she dug into the gravel to run, Brody had her by the waist, squeezing so hard that Ysabel was afraid for her baby. She ceased her struggles immediately, certain she wasn't going to get away this time without grave damage to her unborn child. She'd have to bide her time and watch for another opportunity. For now all she could do was study her surroundings. Darkness surrounded them, lit by the nearby glow of hundreds of lights reflecting off the clouds. They must be close to a refinery or the shipyards. But where?

Green twisted her around and slapped duct tape over her mouth. He did the same for Jenna, zip-tying her hands behind her, as well. Then he marched them farther down the gravel road, surrounded by bushes and tall grasses they couldn't see over. They rounded a curve in the dirt path and stopped behind a maintenance van.

Green slid the rolling door upward and shoved Jenna in first with such force that she slid across the metal floor and banged into the stack of boxes inside. She lay still, her eyes closed, her body limp.

Afraid he'd hurt her baby, Ysabel stepped toward the truck. "You don't have to push. I'll get in." As she stepped up into the van, a hand slammed between her shoulder blades, sending her sprawling forward. With her hands cinched behind her back, she had no way to break her fall. At the last minute, she twisted, landing on her side to avoid injury to her abdomen. Her hip hit the hard metal floor, shooting shards of pain throughout her body. Her vision blurred as she slid into Jenna's soft body. With every bit of effort she could muster, she fought the blackness. She could not afford to pass out. Not with a nutcase ready to blow up her and everybody in Houston. Despite her best attempt, darkness consumed her.

When she came to, the van rumbled to a stop.

Muffled voices barely penetrated the thick metal walls. Ysabel tried to scream, but the engine revved and the vehicle moved forward. She banged her heels against the floor, trying anything to make enough noise to attract attention.

At last, the van stopped and the door slid up and Brody Green's deep voice filled the interior. "Last stop, ladies."

JACKSON took a turn too fast, struggling to maintain control of the truck. Headed east on the Pasadena Freeway, almost to the Bayport Terminal, his phone rang again, displaying Agent Fielding's number in the window.

"Jackson, we sent an agent by Green's house. In his garage, we found traces of bomb-making materials and a diagram of the Champion Shipping oil storage facility near the Port of Houston. If he has what we think he has and he gets inside the oil tank yards, he could blow the Port of Houston off the map. If the explosion is big enough, he could cause some major damage to the City of Houston. We've mobilized all of the first responders and the bomb squad. Stay out of the facility, Jackson. You're no good to anyone dead."

"I hear you."

"But you're going to ignore me, aren't you?" Agent Fielding snorted. "I guess if one of my employees was kidnapped, I'd go in as well."

"She's not just an employee," Jackson admitted. "Ysabel is the woman I love." He said it out loud and couldn't take it back. Nor did he want to.

"I thought so. I'm right behind you by about ten minutes. If you could wait, I'll go in with you."

"No can do. But I'll carry my phone. Let me know when you arrive. I'll have it on vibrate."

"The Houston Port Authority is notifying the terminal operators to stop and hold all vehicles entering the oil storage facility."

"What if he's already in?" Jackson pulled onto the road leading to the Champion Shipping oil storage facility, his heart racing the closer he got. For years, he'd fooled himself into believing that amassing a fortune was the most important thing he could do with his life.

With the very real possibility of losing Ysabel, he'd finally come to realize friends and family just might be more important than any monetary gains. He'd trade all of his fortune to save Ysabel. Every last cent. As he pulled up to the guard house, he was met with a security guard, gun pulled, ready to shoot. The man stood firm, his short hair and solid bearing bespoke a prior service commitment. Jackson liked to hire prior military personnel to guard Champion Shipping facilities. They had the stamina and strength to stand up to anything.

"Step out of your vehicle," the guard demanded.

Jackson dropped down, his hands held high. "I'm Jackson Champion. If you'll let me get my badge out, I'll prove it."

"Slowly, I have my finger on the trigger and I'm not afraid to shoot."

"I believe it." Jackson eased his wallet from his back pocket and removed his badge, holding it out for the guard.

After inspecting the picture and Jackson's face carefully, the guard lowered his weapon but didn't put it away. "Mr. Champion, glad you're here. Maybe you can explain the terrorist alert we received."

"It's just that. We have a potential terrorist threat and we think he might be aiming for this facility. Have any vehicles passed through this gate in the past couple of hours?"

"I just came on duty. Let me check the log." He ran inside the guard booth.

Jackson followed.

The guard booted the computer screen and logged in. "Yes, twenty minutes ago, a maintenance van drove through." The guard shot a glance at Jackson. "You don't think…"

His heart squeezed tightly in his chest. "Yes, I do. Open the gate. I'm going in."

"Yes, sir!"

As Jackson jogged toward his truck, he called out over his shoulder, "The cavalry will be arriving any minute. Let the bomb squad through. I'm afraid we're going to need them."

"You sure you don't want me to go in with you, sir?"

"No, I need you to man the gate in case the van or anyone comes out before I do."

"Yes, sir!" The guard popped to attention and saluted before he remembered he wasn't in the military anymore. His face red, the man hit the gate release button.

Jackson blew through the opened gate, leaving the stunned guard pacing, his gun drawn.

He hadn't gone very deep into the maze of oil storage tanks when he found the van, the rear door open, the interior empty.

The hum of the harbor and the nearby container yards drowned out smaller sounds. Jackson shut down his engine. Much as he'd like to drive through the oil storage yard, he couldn't risk Ysabel's life on rash movements.

He set his shift into Neutral, pushed his truck out of sight of the van and climbed down, reaching beneath the seat for his older, trusty Glock, since his SIG Sauer had become a property of the state in the murder of Stephan Kenig. He knew how to use the gun, had spent a lot of time out at the ranch practicing with Flint and Akeem, each becoming expert with their choice of weapon. But he'd never had to shoot at a man.

His jaw tightened. If it came down to Ysabel or Green, he'd shoot the man in a heartbeat.

He returned to the van, popped the hood and yanked the wires to the electronics. Without serious work, the van would go nowhere.

Jackson eased around the first large storage tank, his eyes adjusting quickly to the darkness, the only light the glow coming from the container yard and the security lights on the corner fences. Long shadows around the base of the tanks could hide not one but a dozen men.

The clang of something hitting metal echoed through the tank farm, making it difficult for Jackson to pinpoint. He left the shadow of the first tank and ran across an opening to the next, careful not to scuff the gravel, thus giving away his position.

Another clang bounced off the towering holding tanks, this time sounding closer.

Checking the alleys at the corner of four tanks, Jackson took a breath and held it, listening for anything—a voice, a footstep, breathing. But the hum of machinery and generators in the distance, drowned out the softer, more subtle sounds. He let his breath out and ran kitty-corner to the tank diagonal from him, he hoped in the direction of the clanging noise.

As he slid around the shadowed side of the tank, he could see the next tank and the ladder snaking upward around the metal cylinder. At the base of the ladder, someone stood straight and unmoving.

For several long seconds, Jackson stood quietly studying

the dark figure. Then it moved a foot, banging it against the metal railing of the ladder. A small foot. A gentle breeze lifted a lock of hair, blowing it across the person's face.

Jackson sucked in a breath. "Ysabel." He was halfway across the open space between the storage tanks before he remembered that there was a killer on the loose in the tank farm. He could have set a trap for him, waiting for just such a moment to take out Jackson Champion. The thought only slowed him for a second. He didn't care whether he lived or died, but he'd be damned if he'd let Ysabel die on his watch.

Her eyes widened and she shook her head violently, her voice muffled by a thick length of silver duct tape over her mouth. Tears glistened in her eyes and on her cheeks.

Anger surged through Jackson. Brody Green was going to pay for this.

He reached for the ropes tying her to the staircase. Before he could lay a hand on them, she kicked his shin.

"Ow!" Jackson stared down at her and dropped his voice. "Why did you do that?"

"Mmm mmmttthh," she said through the tape.

"I'm sorry, Izzy, I can't understand you." He reached out and grabbed the end of the duct tape, easing it off her face, hating how much it must hurt.

When he got it off halfway, she said, "Rip it."

Startled by her demand, his hand jerked the tape the rest of the way off.

Ysabel gasped, more tears falling. "Don't touch me, Jackson."

"I have to get you out of here. Green's going to blow up the place." He reached again for the ropes crisscrossing her body.

"No, Jackson! He's going to blow up this place using me. Just leave."

"What do you mean?"

"If you move that rope, the explosives will go off. You can't save me, Jackson." Her voice broke and she gulped. "Save yourself."

"I won't leave you." Without touching her, he peered behind her. As she'd said, a metal box with wires was tied to the ropes holding her in place. What looked like a lump of clay was stuck to the side of the box. Plastic explosives. His blood chilled.

"Green's still here and he has Jenna. I think he took her to the next row of tanks. You have to help her if you can."

"I won't leave you," he repeated. Frustration overwhelmed him. Jackson was a man who liked to take charge, grab the bull by the horns and to hell with the consequences. But Ysabel's life was on the line and he could do nothing.

Ysabel's tears stopped flowing and she drew in a deep breath. "I'll be okay, Jackson. Find Jenna and see if you can get her out first."

"But—"

"Please. Just go."

Jackson cupped her face in his hand. "I'll be back. I promise."

"No." She shook her head. "You have to find Jenna and get out. Green's got enough explosives here to blow a new channel in the Port of Houston. Get out and warn the rest of the city."

"I'm going, but I *will* be back. You're not getting rid of me that easily, sweetheart." He leaned down and captured her mouth with his, the moment bittersweet. When he broke off the kiss, he pressed his lips to her temple, breathing in the scent of her shampoo. "I love you, Ysabel."

Then he turned and left.

Ysabel dropped the pretense and let the tears flow. "Please, Jackson, save yourself," she sobbed quietly. Her belly tightened, reminding her she'd never told him about his baby, and still couldn't. Jackson wouldn't leave knowing Ysabel was carrying his child and he had to leave to save himself and Jenna.

Afraid to move her arms or hands and set off the bomb earlier than the twenty minutes Detective Green had set on the timer, Ysabel stood straight and still, wishing she'd been smarter and fought harder to get free of Detective Green. Her baby deserved to live.

If she got out of this alive, her first task would be to tell Jackson about their baby. Getting out alive was the big IF.

Chapter Sixteen

After putting a tank between himself and Ysabel, Jackson crouched in the shadows and flipped open his cell phone, speed-dialing Agent Fielding.

"Did you find her?" Fielding answered.

"Yeah. How soon 'til the bomb squad gets here?"

"Fifteen minutes, tops."

"That might be too late. Tell them to hurry. Green has Ysabel wired to the bomb." His voice caught on the lump in his throat. Ysabel had been so vulnerable and brave. He refused to let her die.

"Jesus. I'm almost there. What about Green?"

"I haven't located him yet, but I disabled his escape vehicle. He won't get far."

"Good. See ya in a few." Fielding rang off.

Jackson wove between the tanks until he spied another figure tied to the stairs snaking around the side of a tank. Her long blond hair glinted in the pale light, hanging down over her face.

Even though he didn't love her, he couldn't leave Jenna to die. With time so precious, Jackson spared a moment to scan all directions, straining to see into the shadows. Then he ran across the open space to Jenna. She dangled in the ropes, unconscious, but her chest rose and fell steadily. Jackson checked the ropes binding her to the stairs. No bombs.

He pulled a knife from his pocket and sliced through the ropes. Jenna fell into his arms and moaned.

"It's okay, Jenna. I've got you now." He lifted her into his arms and carried her back toward Ysabel.

"My brother…" she muttered. "He's going to kill me and Ysabel."

Jackson's lips firmed into a straight line, his hands tightening on Jenna's legs. "Not if I can help it."

He ducked into the shadows and eased around the tank Ysabel was tied to until he could see her, standing so still and scared.

A shadow moved at the base of another tank.

Jackson set Jenna on the ground. "Shh. Stay down and close to the tank so that no one can see you. I think I've found your brother."

Jenna grabbed his arm, her face pale in the moonlight. "Be careful, Jackson. He's a monster."

Anyone who would tie bombs to a woman in the middle of an oil-tank farm was a certifiable psychotic. "I know. Stay."

Before he could get to Ysabel, the moving shadow broke free at the base of the oil storage tank and ran across the opening, straight toward Ysabel.

Brody Green grabbed a handful of Ysabel's hair and yanked back her head. "Tell him to give me his truck keys," he demanded, his voice coarse and gravelly.

"No."

"Tell him or I'll shoot you now." He pressed the pistol he was holding against Ysabel's forehead.

Fighting the urge to charge out and kill Green with his bare hands, Jackson leveled his pistol on the man and called out from the shadows, "Let her go." He couldn't fire until he got a clear shot, otherwise he'd risk hitting Ysabel or the oil tank behind her.

"Well, well, the great Jackson Champion finally shows his face." Green tugged on Ysabel's hair, but she didn't cry out. "I would have thought you'd send in your paid minions rather than risk your own rich self."

"Let Miss Sanchez go," Jackson said in a low, clear voice.

"Now then, you know I can't do that. Maybe if you hadn't sabotaged my van, I'd have left and you wouldn't be choosing between your truck and your girlfriend."

"She means nothing to you, Green. Let her go. Your bomb will make a big enough splash with the media without tying her to it."

"Ah, but she means a lot to you, doesn't our Miss Sanchez? She's the reason you wouldn't marry my sister, wasn't she?"

"No, she's not, but that doesn't matter now, does it? I know you're not smart enough to dream up an attack like this all by yourself, Green. Who paid you to blow up the tank yard? I'll double what he's paying you to let her go and I promise you safe passage to the border of Mexico."

"You think I'm fool enough to trust you to keep any promise? Give me the keys to your truck or I shoot her now and save her from being blown to bits in the blast."

"You can have the keys. Take the truck, just leave Miss Sanchez." Jackson took the keys out of his pocket and tossed them through the air to land at Green's feet. "Take them." Then he quickly stepped out of the position he'd been in so that Green couldn't get a bead on him based on the trajectory of the keys and the direction of his voice.

Green pointed his gun into the shadows. "No funny business, Jackson."

"I wouldn't dare."

"Good, because I don't have any qualms over shooting a woman."

Jackson's teeth clenched. "Or beating them up, right?"

"So you found Jenna, did you? That woman is too stupid to live. I should have shot her a long time ago."

Ysabel snorted. "Pleasant thoughts for a brother, don't you think?"

"Shut up." Green punched Ysabel in the face. Then pointing the gun at her head, he bent low to retrieve the keys Jackson had thrown.

While Green bent over, Ysabel kicked out, catching the man's gun hand with her foot. "It's not nice to hit women."

His weapon flew through the air and dropped several yards away.

"Freeze, Green. Or I swear I'll blow your butt from here to eternity."

"Bitch!" Brody stumbled and fell to his knees.

"This is for Jenna." Ysabel swung her foot again, landing another blow to Green's temple, sending him facefirst into the dust.

"And don't call me bitch," she said, her voice strong, despite her potentially deadly position.

Jackson's chest swelled. She was beautiful, even facing death. But he didn't have time to dwell on her stunning performance.

Brody rolled to his side and snatched his gun up into his hand. Then he rolled again, popping up onto his haunches, aiming for Ysabel.

Jackson fired his Glock. The bullet hit Green in the chest, the impact knocking him backward to land with a hard thump in the dirt.

Easing forward, Jackson pointed his gun at Green's head and reached down to check for a pulse. "He's dead."

"Madre de Dios," Ysabel prayed softly. "Where is Jenna?"

"I'm here." The woman stepped out of the shadows and ran to Ysabel. "I'm so sorry for what he did." She stopped short of Ysabel and stared at the maze of ropes and charges. "If only he'd taken me instead of you."

"I'm okay, Jenna. You have to get out of here, now." Ysabel looked to Jackson. "Please, take her out of here. Please."

Jackson grabbed Jenna's elbow. "Come on, you need to get somewhere safe." He reached down and collected his keys from the dirt and ushered her back the way he'd come. When he made it to his truck, he opened it, shoved Jenna into the driver's seat and handed her the keys. "Drive and don't stop until you're out of Houston all together."

The woman shook her head. "No. I won't leave her."

"That's my line." Jackson smiled. "Please, just go."

"You love her, don't you?"

"More than life." He rolled down the window and shut the door. "Now go."

"Okay, but only because I know you'll save her. You're a good man, Jackson Champion. She loves you, too, you know?"

"I hope so, because when this is all over, I'm going to ask her to marry me. Now I have a date with a girl and a bomb."

"God bless you."

Jackson sent a few prayers of his own to the big guy as he jogged toward Ysabel. Before he got to her, his phone vibrated in his pocket. He jerked it out.

"Jackson, I'm at the gate with the bomb squad. We'll be there soon."

"Thanks." Jackson blinked back tears and looked up at the sky. "Thanks." But the day wasn't over until Ysabel was free and the bomb was defused.

YSABEL stood in silence feeling, rather than hearing the silent ticking of her life going away. In the near distance she heard the sound of a truck pulling away.

Tears flowed freely down her cheeks, blurring her vision. He'd gotten away. Thank God, he'd gotten away.

A hand on her arm made her jump. She blinked back her tears.

Jackson stood in front of her, gently brushing away the moisture from her cheeks. "Hey, it's not over yet."

"You're supposed to be gone. Jackson, oh, please, go!"

"I can't." He cupped her chin and smiled down into her eyes. "I want to be with you."

"But you have to go."

"I can't leave the woman I love."

"No, you can't love me. You have to live."

"But I do love you and I won't go until you come with me."

A lump of tears jammed her throat and she swallowed hard to clear the blockage. "I couldn't bear it if you die."

"I'm not going to die and neither are you."

"But the bomb—"

"It's not going to go off." He turned and waved toward a group of men converging on them dressed in heavy padding and shielded helmets. "You see, the cavalry has arrived."

More tears sprang to Ysabel's eyes. "In case they don't get me out of this, I just wanted you to know—"

Jackson frowned. "Save it. You can tell me all about whatever you want to say when we get you out of this."

"But—"

"I won't listen. You and I are going to have a long, *real* talk when this is over. And I don't mean at the pearly gates." He smiled. "Not that I'd be going that direction necessarily. But I don't plan on you or me leaving this world anytime in the near future."

A man dressed like a dark marshmallow stepped up to Jackson and laid a hand on his arm. "Sir, please leave the area while we do our job."

Jackson refused to budge. "I'm not going anywhere without Ysabel."

The man shook his helmeted head. "It's your life, buddy. Just give us room to work."

Stepping back, Jackson stayed close enough Ysabel could see him. "I'm here for you, babe."

"I wish you'd go. I need you to tell my parents, my sister and the rest of my family that I love them. If you don't go, who will tell them?"

"They're *your* family. They deserve to hear it from you. And I couldn't begin to find them all. What do you have, a hundred cousins in the Houston area alone?"

Jackson was cute when he was picking on her. Ysabel hadn't realized how much she'd missed their brand of teasing and she gave him a watery smile. "Something like that. I love a big family."

"I do, too. It took me years to realize it, but that's what I've always wanted." Jackson crossed his arms over his chest, his brows rising in challenge. "Maybe someday we can have one of our own."

Ysabel's chest tightened as hope filled her. "What do you mean?"

The man working on the wires behind her grunted. "Sounds like he's proposing. I hope this is the right wire."

Jackson reached for Ysabel's hand. "I love you, Ysabel Sanchez."

Ysabel smiled across at him. "I love you, too, Jackson Champion." If she died in that moment, she'd die a very happy woman.

A soft snick sounded behind her and she held her breath, waiting for the huge explosion.

Instead the man in the padded gear straightened and held up a wire. "The man was an amateur. This job was too easy." He took off his helmet and smiled at Ysabel. "Which is a good thing for you considering we only had another minute to work with." With a few quick snips, he removed the detonator and the plastic explosives. "You can untie her now. My work is done."

Ysabel sagged, dragging in a deep breath. "It's over?"

"Yes, ma'am. We have a dog searching through the rest of the tank yard to make sure he didn't leave any more presents. But I think Mr. Jackson surprised him before he could arm any more charges."

When the last rope dropped from Ysabel's arms and Jackson had cut the blasted zip tie from her wrists, she stood in front of him. For the second time since she'd known him, Ysabel felt shy and nervous. "Did I really tell you I love you?"

"I heard it." The guy from the bomb squad said. "But then people will say the darnedest things when they think they're going to die. I won't hold you to it."

"But I will." Jackson lifted her hand and pressed a kiss into her palm. "I meant every word I said. And to prove it…" He dropped to one knee.

The blood rushed to Ysabel's cheeks, her heart pounding so hard in her chest she couldn't breathe. She was very afraid she'd pass out and make a fool out of herself before he… Before he what? Dare she hope? *"Madre de Dios."*

Jackson looked up at her in the dim lighting, his own eyes shining and serious. "Ysabel Sanchez, will you marry me?"

"Why?" As soon as the word was out of her mouth, she clapped a hand over her lips.

With a smile, Jackson tugged her hand until she was forced to sit on his one knee. "Didn't you hear what I said not even five minutes ago?"

"The man said he loved you, lady. Isn't that reason

enough?" The bomb squad guy stripped the padding off his chest, shaking his head.

Jackson shot him a glare. "I can handle this, if you don't mind."

The guy raised his hands in surrender. "Right, sorry. Didn't mean to steal your thunder."

"Are you sure?" Ysabel's words came out breathy. She could hardly breathe and quite possibly might hyperventilate.

"More sure than I've ever been about anything in my life." He stood and pulled her into his arms. "Did you mean what you said?"

"About loving you?" Ysabel's chin dipped. "Yes, I've loved you for a very long time."

"And you've been there for me, but I couldn't see you." He tipped her chin up. "I'm sorry I've been so blind."

A tear slipped down her cheek. "You're forgiven."

He touched his lips to hers, but pulled back without kissing her. "Does this mean you'll marry me?"

"Yes." She said. Then throwing her head back, she shouted, "Yes!"

Then he crushed her to his chest and kissed her, his mouth slanting over hers, his tongue delving in to taste hers.

Ysabel's hands slipped up his arms and clasped behind his head, holding him close so that the kiss might last forever.

Inside her blood bubbled, her nerves bounced as though her entire body would light up like firecrackers.

Jackson Champion had asked her to marry him. Her! Ysabel Sanchez.

Then the bubbles burst and her heart fell to her stomach. What would he say when he found out she'd been keeping a secret? A secret she had no right to keep from him?

Ysabel, pushed back from him.

"What's wrong?" he asked, nuzzling her neck and nipping at her earlobe.

"I can't marry you, Jackson."

His head came up, a frown drawing his brows together. "What do you mean you can't marry me? You just said yes."

"I haven't exactly been truthful with you."

"What *exactly* do you mean?" He stared down into her eyes, a smile curling the corners of his lips. "Don't tell me you're already married and I didn't know about it."

"No, no. I'm single all right. With a boss like you, who has time for a social life?" She gave a half-hearted laugh and gulped back another round of tears. "I didn't tell you something I should have told you days ago." She stepped out of his reach and turned her back to him, afraid to see the anger in his eyes when she finally told him.

He reached for her hand and tugged. "You can tell me anything."

Ysabel looked at their joined hands and then up into his eyes. "I'm going to have your baby."

Jackson's frown deepened. "Of course you're going to have my baby. We're going to have half a dozen, if I have anything to say about it. Don't you want children?"

"Oh, yes!" She squeezed his hand. "I meant I'm going to have your baby in exactly seven months."

His eyes narrowed as if he was doing the math in his head, then the brows rose. "You're pregnant?"

Ysabel cringed and answered shakily. "Yes."

Jackson ran a hand through his hair, standing it on end. "You're really pregnant? From that time…"

"Yes and yes." Her nerves stretched to the limit, Ysabel held her breath. "I'm sorry I didn't tell you right away."

He pulled her hand, drawing her closer, his gaze fixed on her belly. "I'm going to be a daddy?" Instead of angry glares and harsh accusations, his words came out softly reverent. Then he looked at her, love shining from his eyes.

If she'd had any doubts, they were wiped away immediately. "Yes, you're going to be a daddy."

His eyes suspiciously bright, Jackson kissed her lips with a gentle brush. "Thank you."

Ysabel laughed, relief making her giddy. "Well, in that case," she pulled him closer, "can we make it a quick wedding?"

"The sooner the better."

"And can I invite my family?"

"Every last uncle, aunt and second or third cousin." He lifted her off her feet and spun her around. "I'll give you the biggest wedding Houston has seen, with more sparkle and bling than all of Tiffany's."

"I don't need a big expensive wedding. I just want you." She cupped his face and kissed him. "But you'll have to be careful, I'm not sure how much roughhousing the baby can take."

"Oh, yeah." Jackson grinned and let her slide slowly down his body. "You concentrate on taking care of Jackson, Jr. and let me take care of the details. I know what, I'll hire a wedding planner."

"That would be lovely."

"How's next week?"

"To meet the planner?" she asked.

"No, to get married."

"Next week?" Ysabel squeaked. "You've got to be kidding."

"Is that too soon?" Jackson's eyes rounded. "I thought you couldn't wait to marry me."

"I can't wait, but a week?" she squeaked again.

"Just leave it to me. All you have to do is show up."

She frowned. "I don't know about this. A man planning a wedding?"

"I went from nothing to worth well over a billion dollars."

He crossed his arms over his chest. "I can do anything I set my mind to."

"I'm sure you can." She ran her hand over his chest, loving that she was free to do it and could do it the rest of her life. "But a wedding? I fear the great Jackson Champion might be in over his head."

He grabbed her around the waist and pulled her into his arms. "Trust me."

Epilogue

"I don't know why I couldn't be out at the ranch to get ready for the wedding there." Ysabel fluffed the satin of her long white wedding dress and tugged at the strapless bust line. "I should have gone for sleeves."

"In this heat?" Delia sat on one side of her dressed in a sea-foam green bridesmaid dress.

On Ysabel's other side Lora Leigh McKade gave a dreamy smile. "I can't wait to see the expression on your face when you see what Jackson's done. It's perfect, just perfect. Oh, and Anna sends her love and congratulations."

"How are she and Katiya?" Ysabel asked.

"Doing fine. Flint, Akeem and Jackson used their clout to give her a new home, a new name and American citizenship. She's going to be fine."

Ysabel smiled. "I'm glad." The poor woman had been through a lot. Thinking about Anna only drew her mind away from her coming nuptials for a minute and the nervousness bubbled right back up in her belly. She drew in a deep breath and let it out. "This is making me crazy. Isn't the bride supposed to plan the wedding? Hand me another cracker will ya, Del? I think I'm getting nauseous."

Delia handed her the entire box. "You better slow down

or you'll be throwing up crackers in your wedding dress." Her sister reached for her hands. "Oh, sweetie, you're shaking."

"I can't seem to help it. Maybe if I'd been in on the planning, I wouldn't be such a wreck."

"Jackson wanted you to be relaxed, not to be troubled about anything." Lora Leigh patted her leg. "He's such a worrywart about you and the baby. It's kind of cute."

Ysabel's lips twitched. "I'm glad he's glad."

Delia snorted. "Glad? The man's ecstatic!"

He was, which filled Ysabel with more happiness than she felt she deserved. Not only was Jackson happy, but he'd also been pushing for her to move in with him even before the wedding.

Needing a little time to get used to the idea and to get her affairs in order, Ysabel insisted on staying in her apartment until after the wedding. She used the excuse that she didn't want to give the paparazzi any more fuel to add to the media circus than they already had.

As they turned onto the road leading to the Diamondback Ranch, Ysabel's palms sweated and butterflies erupted in her stomach. "I'm getting married," she said in a whisper.

Delia hugged her close, brushing a tear from her own eye. "*Sí. Mi hermana* is getting married."

As they neared the ranch house, the cars parked in neat rows on the grass numbered in the hundreds with uniformed security officers directing even more cars to designated positions.

"*Madre de Dios!*" Ysabel raised her hand to her mouth. "He must have invited all of Houston."

Lora Leigh sat back, a smug look on her face. "We had to hire a service to help get the invitations out in record time. Some were hand-delivered. Jackson doesn't do anything in a small way."

Ysabel frowned at the pretty blonde. "You knew and you couldn't have at least warned me? I'm not sure I can stand

in front of all those people, much less walk down the aisle.
It'll take forever!"

With a laugh, Delia patted her hand. "Don't worry, you
can do this. You've been in tougher boardrooms."

The guards waved the limousine down the drive to the
house. Once they came abreast of Flint and Lora Leigh's
home, they could finally see the wedding party.

Ysabel touched a hand to her chest.

The huge expanse of green grass was filled with a big
white tent festooned with garlands of ivy, mixed with red and
white roses. Outside the tent stood row upon row of folding
wooden chairs facing an ornate gazebo, also festooned with
ivy and roses.

"It's beautiful." Tears sprang to Ysabel's eyes.

"I tried to help him with the details, but Jackson insisted
on all of this and then some." Lora Leigh sighed. "I couldn't
have done better if I'd tried. Wait until you see the ice sculptures and the dance floor in the party tent."

"Ice sculptures?" Ysabel couldn't begin to take in all the
tasteful decorations, the people milling about in the shade.
Her gaze panned the crowd, but she couldn't find Jackson.
Panic seized her chest and she feared she'd hyperventilate.
"How did he pull this off in one week?"

Lora Leigh laughed. "The man is driven."

"I'd say he's more than driven," Delia added, her eyes
round in her face as she stared out at the setting fit for a prin-
cess. "He's a human dynamo."

The limousine stopped at the side entry to the large house
and the chauffeur opened the door for the ladies.

Lora Leigh got out first.

When Ysabel stepped out, her knees refused to work. Lora
Leigh grabbed her elbow and braced her until she steadied.

"Come on, we want to do our last-minute primping and
Mama wants to give you something."

"Mama and Papa are here?" Joy welled in Ysabel's heart. "They told me they couldn't make it."

"Oops." Delia grimaced. "That was supposed to be a surprise. Jackson had them flown in from Monterrey on his private jet. You should have seen their faces."

"Come, ladies, let's get this show on the road. There are people waiting in the heat." Lora Leigh herded them into the house and into a large living area, set up as a dressing room for the bride.

A small, thin woman with straight brown hair and green eyes the exact shade of Ysabel's hurried forward, her eyes shining with tears. *"Mija!"* She opened her arms wide and engulfed Ysabel in a tight hug.

"Mama." Ysabel fought to keep the tears from flowing.

"I was so worried when I heard about the bomb. And I couldn't get a flight back because Homeland Security had shut down international flights into and out of Houston."

"You're here now, and that's all that matters. Where's Papa?"

"He's lecturing Jackson." Her mother set her back to look at her in the eyes. "Such a rush. You would think he *had* to marry you."

Ysabel's gaze darted to Delia. "You didn't tell her?"

"Are you kidding?" Delia shook her head. "If I'd told her you were pregnant, all of Houston would know before the sun went down."

"Ysabel!" Another round of exuberant hugging and Ysabel started feeling oxygen-deprived.

Thankfully Delia stepped in. "Mama, please. Jackson is trying to make an honest woman of her. Let her get down the aisle so that he can." She untangled her mother's arms from around Ysabel and ushered her sister to a seat. "Sit, before you fall."

For the next ten minutes, the bridesmaids and mother of

the bride fussed around Ysabel, until she couldn't stand it another minute. Finally, she cried out, "Please let me have two minutes to myself. I need to breathe."

IN another room on the other side of the house, Jackson paced, a cell phone to his ear. He'd considered having it surgically attached after all the calls and preparations he'd made over the last week. This wedding would be perfect if it killed him getting there.

"Exactly where are you?" he demanded into the phone. The jeweler hadn't arrived with the custom-fitted ring and diamond necklace Jackson had ordered to be delivered for the wedding.

"Oh, thank goodness, we're on the drive to the house now," the man answered and hung up.

Jackson glanced at his watch. The wedding began in ten minutes. He barely had time to get the necklace to Ysabel before she made her entrance.

Flint pounded his back between his shoulder blades. "Breathe, man, before you fall flat on your face."

"I am breathing, damn it." He stopped and dragged in a deep breath, realizing for the first time he had been holding his breath.

"If I didn't know any better, I'd say our friend Jackson Champion is having a panic attack," Akeem addressed Flint as though Jackson wasn't in the room.

"For a man who was almost blown halfway to Louisiana, you'd think he could handle one little ol' wedding."

"Little?" Akeem snorted. "Have you been outside? It's a circus out there."

Jackson frowned. "Do you think it was too much? I wanted her to have a fairy-tale wedding. Isn't that what all women want?"

"Not necessarily. Some of them like more subtle displays of love. A quiet ceremony on the courthouse steps is enough."

"Or a quick trip to Vegas for an authentic Elvis wedding." Akeem actually kept a straight face for all of two seconds. Then he was grinning.

"No, really, do you think she'll like it?" Jackson glanced out the window.

Flint nodded. "All kidding aside, you did a great job. Any woman would be happy."

Jackson let out a long slow breath. "She's not any woman. She's Ysabel. And after that scare in the tank yard, I didn't want her to have to do anything but show up."

"Yeah, right. Do you know how hard it is to find a wedding dress in a week? I have it on good authority that it's a nightmare." Akeem grinned. "Taylor came home exhausted every night after shopping with the bride-to-be."

"Same with Lora Leigh," Flint added.

The frown deepened on Jackson's brow. "Had I known, I'd have had a tailor flown in from France to design and sew the damn dress." He glared at the men. "Why didn't you tell me?"

Flint shrugged. "The women made us promise."

Jackson glanced out the front window again. "Did you find out anything about the mysterious man who paid Detective Green to blow up the tank yard?"

"Not yet."

"Green told Ysabel the man was richer than God. What kind of clue is that?" Jackson shoved a hand through his hair and faced his friends. "If we don't find the man behind these attacks, none of us or our businesses are safe." Including his soon-to-be wife and baby. The thought of someone trying to hurt him by hurting them made every ounce of rage burn inside him.

"I hired a man Deke recommended to pick up where your man Tom left off hacking. Unfortunately, what little Tom found has since been expertly brushed beneath the rug. By the way, Tom's here. He threatened all the nurses and doctors so they'd release him in time for the wedding."

Jackson stared out at the drive again. "I've hired a bodyguard for Ysabel. I'd appreciate it if you didn't tell her. She wouldn't be very happy about it."

Flint raised his hand, scout-style. "Wild horses couldn't drag it out of me."

Akeem mimicked Flint. "Same here."

"At least the heat is off the Aggie Four Foundation and Champion Shipping for the time being. Let's hope it stays that way." Jackson studied the black Lincoln Continental inching its way toward the house. When it stopped, he could make out the jeweler's store logo emblazoned in gold lettering on the side panel. "He's here."

"We'll take care of it." Akeem and Flint ran out of the room and returned less than a minute later with a small man in a black suit clutched between them. "Look what we found."

"About time." Jackson strode to the jeweler and held out his hand. "Well, where are they?"

The little man's hands shook as he dug into his suit jacket and pulled out a long flat case. He held it out to Jackson. "I hope these meet with your approval."

Jackson opened the flat box and pulled out a strand of diamonds, a wedding band and diamond engagement ring with a three-carat diamond set in white gold. "I'm not the one who has to approve." He glanced at Flint. "What room is she in?"

"The den on the other end of the house. But it's bad luck to see the bride before the wedding."

"Then you take it." He shoved the necklace into Flint's hands. "Tell her I wanted her to have it and would have given it to her sooner, but well…"

Flint frowned and held out his hand. "Just give me the damned necklace."

"Never mind. I'll deliver it myself." Jackson strode from the room and across the house to the den where Ysabel awaited her cue.

Without knocking he flung the door open. "Ysabel?"

She stood, her long hair swept up on top of her head, curled into loose ringlets. The dress fit her to perfection, her baby tummy not even showing this early in her pregnancy.

Jackson's mouth went dry and his chest swelled to the point he thought his buttons might pop off his shirt and tuxedo jacket.

"It's bad luck to see the bride before the wedding," she said, a smile shining in her eyes.

"You could never be bad luck to me." He stepped through the door and closed it behind him. "I told your mother I'd take care of the something new. I'm sorry I'm late." He stood staring at her, unable to get enough of her. "I've missed you over the last week. Arguing with my new executive assistant isn't as fun as with you."

Ysabel frowned. "What's she like?"

"Temporary. I want you back by my side as soon as possible."

Her frown switched directions. "Good. I don't want to be one of those arm-candy wives who stay home and redecorate because they're bored." She met him halfway and held out her hand. "Something new?"

"New?" He stared down into her moss green eyes, wanting nothing more than to hold her in his arms forever. "Oh, yes." He dug in his pocket. "Turn around."

"Okay." Slowly she turned, the long train on her gown twisting beautifully. She faced a full-length mirror, her gaze finding his in the reflection.

"Close your eyes."

After she'd done as he asked, he slid the diamond necklace around her throat and clasped it in the back. "Okay, you can look."

He stood behind her, staring at her reflection and the look on her face when she opened her eyes.

Ysabel blinked, then her eyes widened. "Are those real?"

Jackson nodded. "Do you like them?"

"Like them?" She touched a finger to the sparkling diamonds, her own green eyes sparkling as bright. "I love them." Then she spun and flung her arms around him.

He kissed her temple and traced a line of kisses to her earlobe. "My baby deserves a little bling, and there's a lot more where that came from." He slipped the engagement ring on her finger.

"*Madre de Dios!* It's huge!" She tipped her hand back and forth, light glinting off the marquis diamond. Then she cupped his face in her hands and stared into his eyes. "I love you, Jackson Champion, whether or not you give me diamonds. You know that, don't you?"

With a smile, he kissed the tip of her nose, then her lips. "I certainly do. That's why I love you so much. You're the real thing, Ysabel, and I want to spend the rest of my life with you."

She leaned up on her tiptoes and kissed him, drawing him into her mouth with all the love she felt. "Then what are we waiting for, cowboy? Are you ready?"

He smiled down at her and gave her his arm. "More than ready to begin the rest of our lives."

* * * * *

*Don't miss the final installment
of* Diamonds and Daddies *next
month. Look for Ann Voss Petersen's*
PRICELESS NEWBORN PRINCE, *where
a few surprises await, only from
Harlequin Intrigue!*

*Celebrate 60 years of pure reading pleasure with
Harlequin®!*

*Step back in time and enjoy a sneak preview of an exciting
anthology from Harlequin® Historical with
THE DIAMONDS OF WELBOURNE MANOR*

This compelling anthology features three stories about
the outrageous Fitzmanning sisters. Meet Annalise,
who is never at a loss for words… But that can change
with an unexpected encounter in the forest.

Available May 2009 from Harlequin® Historical.

"I'm the illegitimate daughter of notoriously scandalous parents, Mr. Milford. Candidates for my hand are unlikely to be lining up at the gates."

"Don't be so quick to discount your charms, my dear. Or the charm of your substantial dowry. Or even your brothers' influence. There are as many reasons to marry as there are marriages."

Annalise snorted. "Oh, yes. Perhaps I shall marry for dynastic reasons, or perhaps for property or influence. After all, a loveless, practical marriage worked out so well for my mother."

"Well, you've routed me on that one. I can think of no suitable rejoinder." Ned rose to his feet and extended his hand. "And since that is the case, let me be the first to wish you a long and happy spinsterhood."

Her mouth gaped open. And then she laughed.

And he froze.

This was the first time, Ned realized. The first time he'd seen her eyes light up and her mouth curl. The first time he'd witnessed her features melded together in glorious accord to produce exquisite beauty.

Unbelievable what a change came over her face. Unheard of what effect her throaty, rasping laughter had on his body. It pounded a beat upon his ear, quickly taken up by his pulse. It echoed through him, finally residing in his stirring nether regions.

So easily she did it, awakened these sensations within him—without any apparent effort at all. And she had called him potentially dangerous? Clearly the intelligent thing for him to do would be to steer clear, to leave her to the tender ministrations of Lord Peter Blackthorne.

"You were right." She smiled up at him as she took his hand and climbed to her feet. "I do feel better."

Ah, well. When had he ever chosen the intelligent path?

He did not relinquish her hand. He used it to pull her in, close enough that he could feel the warmth of her. "At the risk of repeating Lord Peter's mistake and anticipating too much— may I ask if you'll be my partner in battledore tomorrow?"

Her smile dimmed. Her breath came a little faster. His own had gone shallow, as if he'd just run a race—and lost. He ran his gaze over the appealing lift of her brow and the curious angle of her chin. His index finger twitched.

"I should like that," she said.

His finger trembled again and he lifted it, traced the pink and tender shell of her ear, the unique sweep of her jaw. Her pulse leaped beneath her skin, triggering his own. Slowly he tilted her chin up, waiting for her to object, to step back, to slap his hand away.

She did none of those eminently sensible things. Which left him free to do the entirely impractical thing.

Baby soft, the skin of her lips. Her whole body trembled when he touched her there.

He leaned in. Her eyes closed, even as she stood straight against him, strung as tight as a bow. He pressed his mouth to hers. It was a soft kiss, sweet and chaste. And yet he was hot and hard and as ready as he'd ever been in his life.

She drew back a little. Sighed. Their breath mingled a moment before she slowly backed away.

"Oh," she breathed. Her dark eyes were full of wonder and something that looked like fear. He took a step toward her, but she only shook her head. His outstretched hand fell to his side as she turned to disappear into the wood. This was the first time, Ned realized. The first time, since he'd come to the house party at Welbourne Manor, that he'd seen her eyes light up.

* * * * *

Follow Ned and Annalise's story in May 2009 in
THE DIAMONDS OF WELBOURNE MANOR
Available May 2009 from Harlequin® Historical

Available in the series romance section, or in the historical romance section, wherever books are sold.

We'll be spotlighting a different series every month
throughout 2009 to celebrate our 60th anniversary.

Look for Harlequin®
American Romance® in June!

Join us for a year-long celebration of the rugged
American male! From cops to cowboys—
Men Made in America has the hero
you've been dreaming about!

Look for

The Chief Ranger

by Rebecca Winters, on sale in June!

Bachelor CEO by Michele Dunaway	July
The Rodeo Rider by Roxann Delaney	August
Doctor Daddy by Jacqueline Diamond	September

Do you crave dark and sensual paranormal tales?

Get your fix with Silhouette Nocturne!

In print:
Two new titles available every month wherever books are sold.

Online:
Nocturne eBooks available monthly from **www.silhouettenocturne.com**.

Nocturne Bites:
Short sensual paranormal stories available monthly online from **www.nocturnebites.com** and in print with the Nocturne Bites collections available April 2009 and October 2009 wherever books are sold.

Silhouette

nocturne

www.silhouettenocturne.com
www.paranormalromanceblog.com

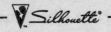

SPECIAL EDITION

FROM *USA TODAY* BESTSELLING AUTHOR

MARIE FERRARELLA

THE ALASKANS

LOVING THE RIGHT BROTHER

When tragedy struck, Irena Yovich headed
back to Alaska to console her ex-boyfriend's
family. While there she began seeing his brother,
Brody Hayes, in a very different light. Things
were about to really heat up. Had she fallen
for the wrong brother?

*Available in June
wherever books are sold.*

REQUEST YOUR FREE BOOKS!

2 FREE NOVELS PLUS 2 FREE GIFTS!

◆ HARLEQUIN®

INTRIGUE®

Breathtaking Romantic Suspense

YES! Please send me 2 FREE Harlequin Intrigue® novels and my 2 FREE gifts (gifts are worth about $10). After receiving them, if I don't wish to receive any more books, I can return the shipping statement marked "cancel." If I don't cancel, I will receive 6 brand-new novels every month and be billed just $4.24 per book in the U.S. or $4.99 per book in Canada. That's a savings of close to 15% off the cover price! It's quite a bargain! Shipping and handling is just 25¢ per book*. I understand that accepting the 2 free books and gifts places me under no obligation to buy anything. I can always return a shipment and cancel at any time. Even if I never buy another book from Harlequin, the two free books and gifts are mine to keep forever.

182 HDN EEZ7   382 HDN EEZK

Name	(PLEASE PRINT)
Address	Apt. #
City	State/Prov. Zip/Postal Code

Signature (if under 18, a parent or guardian must sign)

Mail to the **Harlequin Reader Service:**
IN U.S.A.: P.O. Box 1867, Buffalo, NY 14240-1867
IN CANADA: P.O. Box 609, Fort Erie, Ontario L2A 5X3

Not valid to current subscribers of Harlequin Intrigue books.

Are you a current subscriber of Harlequin Intrigue books and want to receive the larger-print edition? Call 1-800-873-8635 today!

* Terms and prices subject to change without notice. Prices do not include applicable taxes. Sales tax applicable in N.Y. Canadian residents will be charged applicable provincial taxes and GST. Offer not valid in Quebec. This offer is limited to one order per household. All orders subject to approval. Credit or debit balances in a customer's account(s) may be offset by any other outstanding balance owed by or to the customer. Please allow 4 to 6 weeks for delivery. Offer available while quantities last.

Your Privacy: Harlequin is committed to protecting your privacy. Our Privacy Policy is available online at www.eHarlequin.com or upon request from the Reader Service. From time to time we make our lists of customers available to reputable third parties who may have a product or service of interest to you. If you would prefer we not share your name and address, please check here. ☐

HI09

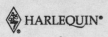 HARLEQUIN®

INTRIGUE

COMING NEXT MONTH
Available May 12, 2009

#1131 HUNTING DOWN THE HORSEMAN by B.J. Daniels
Whitehorse, Montana: The Corbetts
A stuntman who has never given a thought to marriage reconsiders when an adventurous trick rider catches his eye. When a set of incidents on their movie location puts her life in danger, he is determined to catch the culprit...and to get the girl.

#1132 COLLECTING EVIDENCE by Rita Herron
Kenner County Crime Unit
To her, the sexy FBI agent is a perfect stranger. Amnesia has wiped away her memories of their affair...and the crime she witnessed. As her memories return, he must protect her—and the son who may be his—from a killer.

#1133 PRICELESS NEWBORN PRINCE by Ann Voss Peterson
Diamonds and Daddies
Rebels have forcefully overthrown his rule, but when the woman he loves and his newborn son are threatened, the prince must make a choice: fight for his family or the future of his country?

#1134 INTERROGATING THE BRIDE by Carla Cassidy
The Recovery Men
Repossessing a plane is an easy assignment for the former navy SEAL, but the vivacious stowaway in a wedding dress proves to be a problem. Someone is framing her for murder, and he is the only one who can help clear her name.

#1135 KISSING THE KEY WITNESS by Jenna Ryan
When dangerous information about a powerful crime boss falls into the unsuspecting hands of an E.R. doctor, it is a homicide lieutenant who is on call to save her life.

#1136 SAVED BY THE MONARCH by Dana Marton
Defending the Crown
A prince is betrothed to a free-spirited American who wants nothing to do with an arranged marriage. When they are kidnapped, the prince must fight not only for their survival, but also for the heart of the woman he never expected to love.

HICNMBPA0409

www.eHarlequin.com